WISH FOR
A PONY

by

MONICA EDWARDS

Illustrated by Anne Bullen

THE CHILDREN'S PRESS
LONDON AND GLASGOW

This Impression 1968

To
ANN, SHAUN and SHELLEY
who began it

CONTENTS

LIST OF ILLUSTRATIONS

CHAPTER ONE

"More train, Boy," said Diccon stolidly, pushing a yellow chalk into Tamzin's hand. He turned and fixed his gaze on the little blackboard, his blue eyes solemnly expectant.

"It will be the sixteenth train to-day if I do, Dicky. Wouldn't you like a nice horse? Horsy jumping?"

"No horse, Boy. More train comin'." The blue gaze remained steadily fixed on the small space left by a large variety of coloured-chalk trains.

"Well, it's the last one till to-morrow." Tamzin drew a long-funnelled engine with a train of horse-boxes. She worked absent-mindedly and quickly, but when she came to sketching in the horses' heads (rashly looking our of their windows) she took the board down on to her knee and bent over the tiny outlines with sudden interest. At this point Diccon realised that no more was to be gained by staying where he was, and got heavily to his feet with a loud accompanying sigh. "Boy garden, find Daddy," he said, and stumped out by the open door.

Tamzin looked up at his stout departing figure, grabbed the duster, and swiftly transformed the coloured trains into a gently moving cloud of dust about her head. The clean board was set up again on its easel and a white horse's head began to grow from Tamzin's chalky fingers. She hesitated over the ears, rubbed out, drew, rubbed out and drew again. Carefully she went on over the curved back, sketched in a long flowing tail, and arrived at the hind legs. Here she worked laboriously for a long time, rubbing and drawing. Then, "Blow!" she remarked in a disgusted voice, and picking up the board ran out of the kitchen and burst noisily into the sitting-room where a pair of gently reproachful eyes looked up at her over a half-written letter.

"Mummy, the legs just WON'T come right. They never will."

"Not chalk in here, PLEASE, Tamzin. . . ."

"Oh, all right, Mummy, I forgot. But I wanted to show you. I've been trying to get the hocks right for ages, but they just won't."

"How about having a look at that Arab photograph on the calendar?"

"I have. But he's cantering. Fallada here, is jumping."

"I'll be in the kitchen in five minutes getting tea. Perhaps I can show you."

"Oh, THANK you, Mummy! You ARE a sport. I'll put some things on the tray for you."

Tamzin stuck the board back on its easel in the kitchen, stared at it frowning deeply, and then went over to the calendar on the wall. Turning back to April she found the Arab. No, it was no help. But it was the loveliest, most desirable of horses. She stared at it, poring over every detail and reading for the hundredth time, "Grace and pride of bearing; the incomparable charm of the Arab."

"Tea-tray ready?" said her mother, coming in with an envelope in her hand.

"Oh, Mummy! I quite forgot." Tamzin was downcast. "But I could post that for you!"

"All right then, but buck up. Tea will be ready in ten minutes. Where's Boy?"

"In the garden with Daddy. I won't be a jiffy."

Brown bare legs flashed through the door, tawny

"This is the last till to-morrow."

plaits bobbing on dark green jersey. Mrs. Grey smiled to herself and went into the larder with the big blue tray. This dreamy daughter of hers was so much like she herself had been as a child. A picture slid into her mind of a little five-year-old girl lying sobbing on the floor because the grown-ups wouldn't let her hide the rag-and-bone man's donkey while the harsh old man was at the next-door house. Tamzin was ten, and too old for donkeys. When Mrs. Grey had been ten . . .

Spooning strawberry jam into a small brown bowl, she roved back in her mind to rediscover the ponies of her eleventh year. Other people's ponies they had been, but always there had been ponies. It was like this with Tamzin, too ; always ponies, but always other people's.

Quite the worst part of being poor, thought Mrs. Grey, was that you couldn't buy a pony for a child who loved them as much as Tamzin did. This was much worse than having to wear six-year-old hats passed on by her sister (who illustrated books and liked to be well-dressed) and worse than having to mend Diccon's trousers till there was more patch than trouser. . . .

She could hear his loud advancing voice, coming with Daddy up the path, " Find tea. Chocky drink, Boy. Eggy too."

" Are there eggs? He seems to think so," said Mr. Grey, following Diccon into the kitchen. He was a most unclerical-looking vicar, but didn't take this as a compliment when people told him so.

" I hadn't meant to do eggs, but perhaps we can manage it. There are four in the rack."

" It's a poor score. But I've got two broodies now, and Clover and Tansy are moulting." Mr. Grey handed her the egg-saucepan and fished in the drawer for a bib for Diccon. "August is an awkward time for fowls," he remarked, "but we should have plenty of honey when I've got it all extracted."

A flourish through the door and Tamzin was back, breathless and eager. "Is there time to show me now, Mummy? PLEASE! Just the hind legs; we'll do the rest after tea."

Mrs. Grey put down the large brown teapot and took a white chalk from the box. "You want to get the hocks lower down, like this. We used to say 'a good horse should have his hocks well let-down.' Quite a good expression, don't you think?"

"Yes. I think most horsy ones are. You know, Mummy, I do think it was a marvellous stroke of luck, having a mother who used to teach riding. It's almost half-way to having a real pony of my own. I shall work in a riding-stables when I grow up, too. I might even have one of my own. . . ."

"Yes, you might. Who knows? It depends quite a lot on how much you want to, I dare say. I used to be told people could do almost anything if they really and truly wanted to. Now see, lowering the hocks has shortened the cannon-bone, and the whole thing gets a better shape. You try! I must look at the eggs.

They were still sitting round the pleasant tea-table in the sitting-room window when Tamzin's friend Rissa Birnie tore down the drive, scattering pebbles under bicycle wheels, and hurled herself off at the porch.

"What can be the matter with Rissa?" said Mr. Grey, with one eyebrow higher than the other.

"Most likely nothing," his wife replied, passing tea. "She generally gets about in that fashion."

"May I leave the table, Mummy?"

Mrs. Grey nodded, and Tamzin was gone.

"They do seem to waste a lot of energy between them," Mr. Grey remarked, helping Diccon with his cup of warm milk-cocoa.

"They're at the age for it," said his wife, and she rose to pick up the blue tray.

Rissa, who was rightly named Clarissa but who kept this as quiet as possible, was Tamzin's best friend. They went to school together in Dunsford, and though Rissa actually lived quite near the school she cycled down to Westling Vicarage on most days in the holidays. Both girls shared a single passion— ponies. And with both of them the main use to which brains and tact and energy were put was How and Where to get more riding. They collided in the porch.

"Have you heard?"

"Heard what, Rissa?"

"About the horses on the beach."

"No! What horses? Do hurry up!"

"It's a real riding-school, Tam, come down to Dunsmere Sands for the holidays. They've come from some place inland. John told me, and he ought to know; he says they've rented those sheds behind his house and turned them into stables."

"We must go to-morrow and see!"

"Yes, straight after breakfast, and take sandwiches and things. Swimming gear too. We may as well go in if we're there. Will you be ready if I'm here at nine?"

"Of course, but it will be much quicker for you to cycle down the other side of the river and meet me by the lifeboat house. You save at least a mile from Dunsford."

"I know. I suppose it would be best. All right then, say nine-fifteen at the lifeboat house."

"They're sure to charge at least five bob an hour. Hopeless for me." Tamzin began to be downcast.

"Now look here, Tam, have we ever been able to pay for rides? But do we ever get through a week without one? These people's horses will need to be shod, the same as the Dunsford Dairy ponies do. Perhaps they'll be as pleased as the Dairy is to let us take them. I expect they'll be kept up in stables, so won't need to be fetched like Farmer Merrow's Tinkle, but what about grooming and all the rest?"

Tamzin's face lightened. "Yes, and cleaning tack and fetching hay; there's quite a lot we might do if they'll let us. Then we could earn our rides."

"They'll just have to let us! I expect they'll be only too glad if we're properly polite and tactful." Rissa swung round at the sound of Diccon's trotting feet. "Hallo, Honey-Boy! Come see Rissa!"

"NO Honey-Boy! Boy flying, like bee, like bird!" He lifted his hands, new-washed after tea, and ran tiptoe over the lawn.

"Just look!" said Rissa, who adored him. "Don't pull me, you ass! I like watching Dicky."

"I know, but I want to show you something," said Tamzin, who also adored Diccon but had all day to watch him. "Mummy and I've been doing it in my room. Oh, come ON!"

They went up two-at-a-time in their accustomed fashion to Tamzin's attic-room. "I say!" breathed Rissa on the threshold. "This is smashing!"

"Yes, I thought you'd like it. But we're having the most awful bother keeping them on the wall.

Every time it rains or anything they peel off, and we've tried everything, pretty well. Mummy cut them out of white paper and then Indian inked them. We stuck them up first with paste, then we got some patent gluey stuff, and now we think we'll have to re-distemper the walls and put them all up again afterwards. This distemper's so dusty."

"You simply must get them to hang on somehow. They look marvellous all round the wall like that. Did you trace them?"

"Yes. Don't you recognise the Arab from the kitchen calendar? And those hairy shires from the *Farmer's Year* that Farmer Merrow gave us? This one came from my *Practical Horsekeeper*—you know, that used to be Mummy's."

"M'm. The black of them stands out perfectly on your creamy walls. I do wish mother would let me do things like this in my room. But you know how she likes it kept."

"Yes, I know. Pink and dove-grey and muslins. It IS pretty, but . . ."

"There's something about being able to do your own room how you like. Well—the way you can."

"I want my room to be a horse room, Rissa, when I've done with it. All my pictures are going to be horsy ones, and I want horse book-ends and horse-brasses, and even horse-curtains if I can get them. Say—blue material with galloping white horses on it. Do you suppose there IS such a material?"

"I dare say. But it would be very expensive."

"M'm. That's the whole snag. It'll take me years to get half the things to finish the room. But it will be fun collecting things, and there's Christmas and birthdays. And Mummy has lots of ideas. This frieze was her idea, and she did nearly all of it, though I helped a bit. We'll have to get Daddy to do the distempering, though, because Mummy says Diccon would be SURE to fall into the pail or something if she does it. He never stays far from her for long, does he?"

They stared at the frieze in reflective silence for a moment, then, "Dunsford Gymkhana's at the end of this month," said Rissa.

"Well, I suppose we'll go as usual, and watch as usual."

"Tamzin, you do get GLOOMY! I've an idea, anyway."

"What?"

"Well, don't you think Farmer Merrow might let us ride Tinkle in some of the events? Not the jumping, because she doesn't——"

"Come to that, neither do we."

"I know, cuckoo, but there's the Bending, and they might have 'Walk, Trot, Mount and Gallop.'"

"Yes, and Musical Chairs. It IS an idea. But you have to get him in the mood. He can be most awfully chilling."

"True. The moment must be well-chosen. And we have to have time to practise. Not that we'll be able to get her often enough for PROPER practice."

"Who'll have the rosette if we win anything?"

"Blowed if I know. The owner of the pony, I dare say, IF we win."

Tamzin nodded. "Tinkle is so staid, though she's a darling little mare, and nice to learn on. After all, she was the beginning of everything for us."

Rissa picked herself up from the bottom of Tamzin's bed. "Better be moving. Coming part way?"

"I'll come as far as the wishing gate, if you're

going the field way. Then I can help you lift your bike over."

They clattered downstairs and out to the bicycles. Their way lay through the village, past the church where the verger was locking up for the night, and then through the sheep levels to where the wishing gate marked the approximate midway point to Dunsford. Here the girls dismounted and heaved Rissa's bicycle over the fence beside the gate, after which they solemnly walked through the gate itself, one after the other, with their eyes tightly shut.

"Never tell a wish," said Tamzin, "but I know perfectly well what you always wish, and it's the same as I do, isn't it?"

"Of course. But you mustn't *dare* to mention it, or it will never come true."

"Daddy says it won't anyhow. At least, not because of the gate. He says it's a heathen idea. But one can hardly ask God for a p——, I mean for a THING, can one? Only for things like courage, and being better at sums and all that. Perhaps He doesn't really mind us just wishing at the gate as we aren't superstitious in the ordinary way, are we? I mean, like Mrs. Merrow who won't sit down thirteen at the table, or look at the new moon through glass, or is it in a mirror?"

"I shouldn't worry. To-morrow at nine-fifteen!"

"Yes, and don't forget your swim-suit. AND grub. I shan't have enough for two, and there WAS a time last hols . . ."

CHAPTER TWO

Tamzin was supposed to make her own bed in holidays and at week-ends. Sometimes it would have passed a Girl Guide test, sometimes it was like a rough sea, and sometimes it was completely forgotten. This morning it was like a rough sea and was, moreover, strewn with all kinds of scrambled garments like a jumble sale after the first mad rush. Tamzin had mislaid her swim-suit. It was not in the drawer, either, after all her trouble, and she was about to dash down the attic stairs and look in the airing-cupboard when she heard her mother's voice calling up from the hall, " Be sure to leave everything tidy, Tamzin!"

She gathered up the unruly jumble sale, pushed it harum-scarum into her drawer and banged it shut. A hasty smooth over of the rough sea and then down the banisters to the landing. It was nearly nine o'clock, and her bicycle still to be pumped. In the airing-cupboard, under a pile of variegated underwear, she discovered the swim-suit and bounded downstairs rolling it up in her towel as she went.

Diccon's lost plea, "More train, Boy, chalk, PLEASE !" wafted after her through the back door as she swept up the little lunch packet and disappeared round the dustbin towards the bicycle shed.

At half-past nine she was waiting by the ferry. The little boat was half-way across the river, bringing the District Nurse and her bicycle to Westling village. Old Jim, ferryman at Westling for nearly

forty years, rowed his little green boat with perfection and the least possible expenditure of energy.
Tamzin loved him. To her he was the symbol of
high adventure. He had been all over the world in
his time, and he wore little round brass ear-rings
and high boots turned down below his knees.
Often, when Tamzin was without her bicycle, he
would let her row, even when she was not the only
passenger. She tried valiantly to "feather" in a sea-
manlike way, but the oars were too heavy for her
small arms.

The boat grounded with a crunch on the shingle,
and Tamzin smiled politely at the District Nurse
who jumped out, lifted her bicycle to the ground
and said, "Is your father in, Tamzin? I want to see
him about the meeting to-night."

Tamzin said he was, but was shaving when she
left, and settled herself in the stern of the ferry-boat,
braced against her bicycle saddle.

"Mornin' Miss Tamzin, You after them 'orses,
I'll lay."

"Well, as a matter of fact I *was* going to have a
look at them. How did you know?"

"Knowin' you, an' knowin' they was there."

"You're very clever, Jim."

"I bin about a bit."

Tamzin stared reflectively at the river, rushing
inland in its glassy way. "Funny, but I never quite
get used to seeing the river run the wrong way when
the tide's coming up," she said.

Old Jim grunted non-committally, leaned over to
pick up a piece of floating driftwood, and continued
on his semi-circular course across the swiftly flowing
water. A yard or two from the farther bank he
turned the boat with a skilful counter-movement of

his oars and backed her to the steps. Tamzin grabbed the iron mooring-ring, and Old Jim shouldered her bicycle and carried it up the steps for her.

"Thank you very much, Jim. I'll pay for both ways in case I lose it on the sands. I won't be back till tea-time." She cycled cheerfully along the sandy road singing "D'ye ken John Peel" to tum-te-tum till the lifeboat house came into view round a hump of dune. She was actually there before Rissa and had a minute to wait before the expected bicycle rushed madly round the corner and careered to a sudden standstill.

"Rissa, you're always so FRIGHTfully rushed, I can't help expecting the worst whenever I see you. Though I ought to know by now that it's simply the way you get about."

"No point dawdling. Come on. Got everything?"

"M'm. I think so."

"What're we going to do first?" said Tamzin, cycling with difficulty on the sandy road.

Rissa pondered. "What about a swim?"

"BEFORE the horses?" Tamzin said, aghast.

"We've got all day. They won't be out yet, most likely."

"Suppose we leave our bikes at John's and have a look round first?"

"Oh, all right. Only we shall have to look at his rabbits. . . ."

They turned off the sandy road up a sandier track towards the house of John Starling, who was a junior at Dunsford High School. His mother was a tower of strength on all parish occasions and frequently at the Vicarage, so the girls found it impossible to maintain their usual aloofness-from-juniors attitude towards John, whom they treated more as a younger brother. They found him swinging on the gate.

"I was looking for you," he said.

"Well, here we are. But we might just as easily NOT have been, so you might just as well have been doing something else," said Rissa, not unkindly.

"I knew you'd come the first fine day. The horses are lovely. I can see them looking out of their boxes from my bedroom window. There're five. Bring your bikes to the wood-shed and then you can see my rabbits. One's had young this morning."

"You mustn't look at them with new young!" said Rissa, horrified. "The mother'll eat them if you start disturbing."

"I know *that*! Daddy told me years ago. We aren't going to look at her anyway, only at Flopsy and Patty and Samson. P'raps you can see Mina's young next time you come—if it isn't to-morrow or anything like that."

They wheeled the bicycles into the wood-shed, and Mr. Starling, looking up from pea-picking in the garden, called cheerily across, "'Morning, girls! Going swimming? That's right, push them in the shed with ours as usual. Any time you like."

John was opening the first hutch at the side of the wood-shed, and gently extracting a large Blue Beveren. He held it carefully with one hand under the body. "Did you know it's wrong to hold a rabbit by just only its ears?" he asked. "You really have to help the weight with a hand underneath like this, only lots of people don't know, and it must be awful to be their rabbits. This one's Samson. He's the father of the babies. I must change his water; LOOK what he's done to it!" Samson was lovingly

"*They* are *lovely*," *Rissa said.*

replaced, and his water-dish fished out from under his scattered bedding.

Tamzin and Rissa, who were not really interested in rabbits, bore all this very gently because you mustn't be off-hand with people who are protecting your bicycles for you, and they even worked up a creditable interest in the diet and routine of Flopsy and Patty before saying "Good-bye, see you later," and racing off towards the group of wooden sheds behind the Starlings' orchard. Over the orchard fence across the green track, and they were at the gates of the stable-yard. Rissa glanced up and read, "Hillocks Riding School. First-Class Hunters, Hacks and Ponies Always for Hire."

"Doesn't say how much," said Tamzin.

"Well, what can it matter? If it was only two-and-six we couldn't do it, and it's never less than four shillings. Likely to be much more here as they don't have it on the board."

They leaned on the gate, propping their chins on their arms. Tamzin gave a loud happy sigh.

"M'm. They *are* lovely," Rissa said, staring at the three inquiring heads lifted over three stable doors.

"Two chestnut hunters and a grey pony. Wonder what the other two are."

They looked at the vacant doorways and then back to the three watching heads. "Wonder what the pony stands?" Rissa said. "Difficult to judge height from just the head. Would you say fourteen hands?"

"No. More like thirteen, or even less," said Tamzin, who wasn't as sure as she sounded.

A young woman appeared round the corner of the stables. She wore breeches and carried a saddle and bridle on her arm. The girls smiled tentatively.

She smiled back, called "Lovely morning!" and went into the grey pony's box. Tamzin and Rissa listened with deep and silent interest to the sounds of preparation in the box; the ring of iron shoes as the pony moved over for his saddle, and the jingle of his bit as he settled it in his mouth. The young woman reappeared through the stable door, shut it behind her and went round the sheds again the way she had come. The pony's shapely little head lifted over the door as the latch clicked down, and turned to watch her out of sight.

"Double bridle," Rissa said, and almost at once, back came the enviable one in breeches with a second saddle and bridle. This time she said, "Do you like our horses?" and the girls said, "Oh, YES!" and "We think they're lovely!" at the same time.

The chestnut with the white face was saddled next, and when the girl-groom left his box she came across to the gate and said, "Do you ride?"

"Well, here and there," said Tamzin. "Not like this. Mostly we just take the Dairy ponies to the forge."

"And sometimes we fetch up a pony called Tinkle for a farmer we know, when she's grazing away from the farm."

"We mean to have a proper riding school like yours when we grow up, though," Tamzin added.

The girl in the breeches laughed. "Oh, this isn't MY stables ! I only work here."

"What a shame! We were going to ask you if WE could work here in the holidays to earn riding. I expect the owner is terrifying, and you aren't a bit," Rissa told her.

"Well, you ARE likely to think him a bit austere at first, but he isn't really. We're only here for the holidays, you know. We go back to Tonbridge at the end of September."

"Is he here now?" Tamzin asked, gathering courage. "What is his name?"

"Mr. Randall, and mine's Joan Wade," she smiled. "I'm afraid he's out just now with a boy on the other pony, but they should be back any minute. I have a ride myself at ten with a little girl on Cobweb."

"Cobweb! Because he's grey? How nice! What're the other horses' names?" Tamzin asked.

"The bright chestnut is Carillon, and the one with the white face Allegro. There're the other two, coming up the lane. Mr. Randall's riding Ballerina and the boy's on Sea Pie."

The girls' eyes paid silent homage to the superb white mare coming towards them. She moved like water, fluid and smooth, and she flirted her small hooves on the grassy track, eager for the stable with sweet hay in the rack. It was almost impossible not to watch this perfect combination of splendid horse and graceful rider. Sea Pie, who would have held the eye of any horse-lover when not eclipsed by the mare beside him, came collectedly on, almost completely unnoticed. He was a perfect child's pony, well-mannered, narrow, and with a smooth and balanced action. His mane and tail were black, against a warm bay coat. He struck out his little hooves precisely, and carried himself with pride, though he was but thirteen hands and very young.

They came up to the gate, and the girls held it open for them to pass through. Following behind was a girl in fawn jodhpurs riding a bicycle. She propped it up against the fence and walked with Miss Wade across to the grey pony, Cobweb, extending a piece of apple on the palm of her hand.

Ballerina and Sea Pie coming back.

Ballerina and Sea Pie were led into their boxes as Cobweb and Allegro clattered out of theirs. The two girls, leaning absorbedly on the gate they still held open, watched Miss Wade adjusting stirrup-leathers for her pupil. She held the chestnut's reins over her arm as she worked, and he pushed his muzzle against her pocket, his mind on bits of carrot. She found a piece for both of them, and mounted, followed the girl on the little grey through the gate with a smiling, "Thank you!" for Tamzin and Rissa. The boy who had ridden Sea Pie shot through the gate on a very shiny bicycle as the girls swung it to, and pedalled bumpily down the track.

Ballerina's door clicked, and Mr. Randall stood looking across the yard, her saddle and bridle on his arm.

"Anything I can do for you?" he asked gravely and courteously.

"We were looking at your horses," Tamzin answered shyly, thinking how utterly unapproachable the owner was, and how unmentionable their quest.

Rissa suddenly decided it was now or never, and plunged in with, "We really HAD meant to ask if we could help here in the stables to earn riding. You see, doing things properly isn't possible for us—practically never, I mean . . ." Her voice ran down like a clock that needs winding. Mr. Randall was exquisitely polite.

"I'm very sorry," he said, "but I really don't think we need any help at the moment. Perhaps next time we come," he smiled barely perceptibly. "I'm sorry to have to disappoint you," he said, and went out of sight round the sheds with Ballerina's tackle.

The girls stayed for a second, flicking a good-bye glance to each shining head before turning silently down the grassy track.

"Swim?" said Rissa, after a minute.

"M'm," said Tamzin, without heart.

They trudged over the sand to a hollow in the dunes where they dumped their satchels and began changing. Neither had much to say. Their high hopes were down below ground. They pulled on swim-suits and pushed their hair in rubber caps, Rissa helping Tamzin with her plaits.

Their high hopes were down below ground.

A scramble up the loose sand brought them out of their hollow to the high top of a marram-covered dune where they stood and looked out over the fine stretch of sand to the sea.

"Tide's a bit low for a good swim. Never mind, must do something," Rissa said.

They spotted Cobweb and Allegro trotting through the Cut between the dunes and on to the sand. Nothing was said, but they watched the horses canter collectedly towards the sea as they themself took a parallel path for their swim.

"Shan't stay in long," Tamzin said. "Tide's not high enough."

"No, we'll go in again later."

They swam dispiritedly about. There were no waves to surf-ride on, and the water was not deep enough for duck-diving, which they usually liked to practise for the Royal Life Saving Society's bronze medal examination. They were both entering for this with others of their school when the autumn term began.

"I'll be drowned if you like to practise artificial respiration on me," Rissa said, suddenly making an effort to cheer the easily cast-down Tamzin.

"All right; lie down then."

Rissa flopped on her front on the wet sand. "Don't tickle," she said.

Tamzin knelt astride the limp figure and placed her hands squarely on the wet back, just over the lungs, thumbs parallel, fingers spread. She leaned back, swung forward with sturdy pressure and began counting, "ONE, two ONE, two . . ." in time to her rhythmic pressure and release.

"Ow! You're tickling!" Rissa burst out.

"'M not. Can't help it, anyway. Keep STILL . . ."

"You ARE! Stop it, you ass——"

The practice broke up violently with Rissa rolling uproariously over, laughing loudly and tippling Tamzin sideways. They got up, feeling a little lighter hearted, and padded towards the dunes.

"'S going to be awful, drying with all this sand on us," Rissa remarked.

CHAPTER THREE

DRESSED, but rather sandy still, the girls sat on the crown of their dune drying hair. Rissa's was a rich brown, shoulder length and slightly curly. She was growing it; a thing she did about once every two years but generally gave up in despair at the half-way stage "because it tickled." Tamzin was looking at it now, and said encouragingly, "I don't believe you've EVER got quite as far as this with your hair before."

"Haven't I? It nearly came off at half-term, only Uncle Bill came and took me to Hastings for the day."

"If you stick it a bit longer there'll soon be enough for plaits. Then you'll be over the worst."

"M'm. But it's terrible getting there. Tickles so. I don't expect I'll bear it."

"RISSA! LOOK!" Tamzin leapt to her feet, staring inland over the waving grass.

"It's Carillon!" gasped Rissa. And Carillon it was, galloping wildly towards the Cut in the dunes, something dreadful thumping and whacking at his heels, maddening him with fear and apprehension.

"Got his hitching post on the end of his halter-rope. Easily break his legs. Rissa, quick, what'll we do?"

"Try to stop him somehow. Run——"

They ran, stumbling and gasping for breath, towards the Cut.

"May stop at the fence," gulped Rissa.

Carillon didn't stop. He jumped the fence, his post whanging on his hocks as he came down. The

"Try to stop him somehow.   Run——"

girls half-paused, terrified lest the horse should falter and hang a broken leg. He galloped on. He was a bare two-hundred yards away now, and between them and him was a four-foot post-and-rail fence.

"He MUSTN'T jump that, MUSTN'T——" said Tamzin, nearly crying, and they felt their lungs were bursting with the strain of their last spurt.

Rissa, the elder, was there first and scrambled over, Tamzin on her heels. They had fifty yards to spare, and ran on to meet the terrified horse, no room in their burdened minds for thought of personal and serious danger to themselves. They called his name sharply, "Carillon! Carillon! STAND!" and "Steady old horse!" as they slowed and spread their arms, straight in his path.

He came like a thunderbolt, nostrils flared, eyes

fixed. Tamzin shut her eyes momentarily ; "This is the end," she thought in her numb mind, but she flicked them open to see the sweat-streaked chestnut slither to a trembling standstill, so near that she could feel his breath.

"Steady, old horse!" she said again, not believing it, extending a gentle hand to his head. She was holding his halter and he was lowering his head to her touch. She soothed him with soft words and softer fingers, while Rissa worked desperately at the knot in the rope. The post must be released before he made the slightest movement. The tips of Rissa's fingers bled, but she worked on until the knot was loosed. The horse stood quietly. He trembled violently and steamed where the August sun fell on his soaking skin.

Tamzin led him gently a few steps from the loosened post so that he might not see the dreadful thing again and, looking up, saw Mr. Randall hurrying towards them across the field. Other people had begun to collect in twos and threes along the road and on the dunes, staring at the girls and the horse.

Carillon pushed a shivery muzzle towards his master, who took the halter from Tamzin's hand and caressed the chestnut head.

"You did well," he said quietly, looking at the two girls. "You probably saved his life. If he had jumped the second fence he might have landed on the post."

"We didn't really do very much," Tamzin said. "It was his sense in stopping when he did."

"I think you did very much indeed," Mr. Randall said, with his shadow of a smile. " You ran till you nearly burst to save him, and you reassured him with words he knew. He was so frightened that he stopped at the familiar words, believing they meant help. And you were calm and didn't make a fuss to upset and scare him more."

"I didn't feel calm," Rissa said honestly, "but I did try to look as if I was. I was pretty scared, really." She looked down, feeling a little ashamed of this.

Tamzin said, "I was just about frightened to death," in a little slow whisper. She felt it was a disgraceful admission, but Rissa had been so honest she must say so too.

Mr. Randall, walking Carillon towards the road, said, "Bravery is doing something you're badly frightened about. You don't need courage if you aren't afraid."

At the road Rissa said, "We go this way. Good-bye."

Mr. Randall smiled, "Good-bye! Will you come and see us to-morrow? To ask after Carillon? There'll be a lot to do you know, with these legs to mend. Poor old fellow! He's going to be lucky if he gets away with it."

"Yes, of course we will," the girls said. "First thing in the morning. Good-bye!"

They walked up John Starling's garden path, feeling a little limp after the high excitement of the past half-hour. John heard the gate and rushed round the house to meet them.

"There's just been a most awful thing happen at the riding school," he said, "an' I saw it all because I was in the orchard picking rabbit leaves."

"Go on," said the girls, who had no idea how the matter had begun. When they had left the stables Carillon had been quietly standing in his box.

"It was all because of Mr. Murphy's donkey. You know, in the field next to the stables. Mr. Randall took a horse from the stable into the yard and tied him to a post so's he could mend the stable door. Well, he was hammering it. Then Mr. Murphy's donkey brayed like anything, and the horse threw his head up; I think he didn't like it. The awful thing was, the post came out of the ground——"

"It IS sandy," Rissa said.

"—and that frightened him more than ever and he reared up, and then before Mr. Randall could reach him he'd jumped sideways over the little fence, post and all, and galloped down the track. The post was banging at his legs and it was awful. Mr. Randall ran down the track after him, but he'd never be able to catch him. Did you see him or the horse or anything, on your way up?"

"Well, yes. We walked to the road with them, actually. He had the horse," Rissa said cautiously, being anxious to terminate the conversation, pick up the lunch packets from the bicycle saddle-bags and get away before John thought about his rabbits again. Both girls were hungry; it seemed years since their breakfast.

"Gee whizz!" John said. "What could have stopped him? He was galloping ALL OUT! I'm going to see! Good-bye!" He ran along the orchard path intent on discovery.

"Well, saved from the rabbits THIS time," Tamzin said. "Come on, here's your lunch packet."

They walked back across the field towards their hollow. Tamzin kicked the abandoned hitching-post as they passed it. "Beastly thing!" she said, with feeling.

"Yes! Poor old fellow! He was just as frightened

as we were," Rissa said. "Wonder what would have happened if he HADN'T stopped?"

"Mowed us down, I suppose," Tamzin said, with a little shiver.

"M'm. Would've been nasty. Miss Wade was right about Mr. Randall though, wasn't she? He was MUCH nicer after the post affair than when we first saw him."

"Yes. And I liked the way he stroked Carillon's face. As if he really loved him; not just kept him to make money with."

They reached their hollow in the dunes and stretched out on the warm sand, unwrapping packages and making pillows of bathing-towels.

"You've got an egg!" said Rissa. "Lucky thing!"

Tamzin unwrapped a snow-flecked brown egg from a page of the *Daily Telegraph*. "You should keep chickens," she said.

"Mummy says they're messy."

"They are. But if you don't have mess you don't have eggs—'cept shop ones. Have half of mine."

"Oh, THANKS! You can have half my sausage." They swopped.

"Funny, the names they give race-horses," Tamzin said, poring over the egg-wrapping, her mouth full of sausage and egg mixed. "There's one here called ' Head On.'"

"Funnier if it was off," Rissa said.

"Ass!" said Tamzin, tolerantly. "There's one called ' Nice Day.' Oh, and ' Safety Pin,' of all the balmy ideas."

"Let me look!"

Tamzin passed the crumpled paper over and stretched lazily in the sun, munching happily and staring at tiny, cotton-wool clouds.

Bathing Carillon's hind legs.

"What'll we call our ponies, if we ever get them?" she said.

"What about Tamara?" Rissa mumbled, through half a sandwich.

"Sounds like someone who can't say 'to-morrow.' Looks nice in print though," Tamzin conceded.

"Well, what about yours? Fallada, I suppose, like the one you're always drawing."

"Not unless he's white. I think my pony will be 'Woodwind.'"

"M'm. Which sort? Wind in the woods kind, or orchestral kind?"

"Either. Both."

They chewed in silence for a bit.

"Mummy said I could bring you back for tea," Tamzin offered, folding empty paper bags.

"Thanks! Mine won't mind. She said I could stay if I liked."

They shut their eyes and basked contentedly in the warm sunshine, giving food a chance to settle down before their swim.

Meanwhile, at Hillocks Riding Stables, Mr. Randall and Joan Wade were busy bathing Carillon's battered hind legs in preparation for the vet's arrival. The horse stood quietly with his head hung low. "I believe he knows we're helping him," Miss Wade remarked, straightening her back and stroking the smooth quarters.

"Yes, I have a great respect for his intelligence. It was that, of course, that saved him, and probably saved the girls as well. They'd have had a poor deal if he hadn't stopped, the plucky blighters."

"Yes, they were plucky. Or do you suppose they didn't realise the danger?"

"They realised it all right. Bravest thing I ever saw. And so sensible." He moved the bucket of warm water to the yard and dried his hands.

"Better roll a bandage round that lot till the vet arrives. Girls are coming out in the morning to ask after the horse. I may not be here—thought of boxing Carillon back to Tonbridge and leaving him with George—but make them welcome; they've sense enough to be around stables. Oh—and see they get some riding." He walked towards the saddle room for bandages, and Joan Wade picked up the bucket and emptied it with the ghost of a smile.

The girls found the tide well up when they went down for their second swim. They were in high spirits and rollicked through their life-saving practice like a pair of irresponsible porpoises.

Rissa contrived to be tickled again while being towed on her back and engulfed Tamzin in a whirl of bubbles and green water.

"Your fault!" she shouted joyously. "Ought to be able to hold 'em wriggling."

Tamzin came up blowing like a baby whale, grabbed Rissa by the shoulders and with a mighty shove put her under the water.

"Worm!" she said, cheerfully.

They spent about half an hour in this fashion before rubbing down, dressing, and setting out across the now historic field for their bicycles.

No one was about at the Starlings, so the girls went round to the back door and found Mrs. Starling's ' girl ' cleaning silver.

"They've gone to Dunsford, shopping," she told them.

Setting out across the now historic fields

Rissa said, "We're just taking our bicycles. Will you say Thank you for us, please? Good-bye!"

"Good-bye, Miss! Oh, and Master John said to tell you you can look at his rabbits if you like."

The girls exchanged glances, and Rissa called back, "I don't think we will, without John. Just in CASE anything happened, you know. Good-bye!"

"Wish something *would* happen!" Tamzin said, with feeling, as they cycled uncertainly down the winding path.

Rissa said, "Don't be horrid!" in shocked tones, and Tamzin grumbled back, "They lose us *hours*."

"Well, they won't to-morrow. We can leave our bikes at the stables."

Old Jim saw them from his hut on the Westling side of the ferry, and walked down to his boat. The girls sat on the lowest step and waited.

"Got a loose tooth," Tamzin said, wriggling it with her tongue, "molar, I think."

"Lend me twopence?" Rissa said, disregarding.

"Can't. Have to owe it. Jim won't mind."

"No, I suppose he won't. He's nice, isn't he! Do you think it's true about his smuggling when he was younger?"

"Shouldn't wonder. Some people say there's smuggling going on even now on this coast, in a smallish way."

"TAMZIN!"

"True. I heard Daddy telling Mr. Rogers so last Sunday after evensong. He said he wouldn't be surprised if someone got caught red-handed one moonlight night."

"Golly! Well I hope I'm there when they are!"

The boat slid stern-first to the steps, and Old Jim

kept her steady with his oars while the girls jumped in.

"Do you mind if we owe for Rissa, Jim?"

"Next time will do, Miss Tamzin. Won't worry me. Found they 'orses?" he twinkled.

"Yes. Well, I mean—we're going again to-morrow."

"That 'ere chestnut's legs bad 'urt, eh?"

"Chestnut? Who told you?" Tamzin's jaw dropped. "You don't mean you know about——?"

"Know? Course I knows. So does yer pa. An' yer ma too, 'n all the village be now, I'll lay."

"Oh, JIM! What a tragedy! We're sure to be stopped going if they think we're being rash. How COULD it have got about? I'd meant to explain it all so CAREFULLY to Mummy, later. You know, at a good moment."

"News is winged, Missy. I've rowed six parties over from Dunsmere sin' dinner, and they never let no grass grow under none of their feet."

The girls stepped out of the boat and walked along the shingly road to the Vicarage in anxious silence.

Diccon, who was wiggling his fingers under a dripping tap in the scullery, came rushing to meet them. Rissa gathered him up endearingly and they walked into the kitchen. Mrs. Grey was cutting bread and butter at the table. She looked up and said, "Your fame has been travelling before you!" Then, seeing their apologetic faces, "Well, you don't need to look ashamed about it!"

"We were afraid you'd think we'd been rash. Only really, there wasn't time to think about it much, beforehand. It all happened so quickly."

"Perhaps you were rash; perhaps you weren't.

It depends how you look at it," Mrs. Grey said, spreading butter. "And we haven't heard YOUR account yet. But there's a thread of rashness in most kinds of courage, and I think the courage generally justifies the rashness." She smiled, stacking slices on a blue and white plate.

Tamzin shot her an adoring glance and Rissa said, "Can we carry those in for you?"

CHAPTER FOUR

DRESSING in the morning, Tamzin wandered into her mother's room, still at the vest and knickers stage and with a scarlet tooth in her hand.

"It IS a molar, Mummy," she said. "My first. Can I have twopence for it, should you think?"

"PENNIES for teeth," Mrs. Grey murmured through a mouthful of hairpins. She wore her thick brown hair in a plaited crown round her head; a style Tamzin loved.

"But as it's a DOUBLE tooth, Mummy?"

"Double pay for double teeth?" Mrs. Grey smiled, twisting under the end of a plait, "That's a new one on me!"

"Oh, all right. I only thought I'd ask. Where's Diccon?"

"Gone downstairs with Daddy. He was being a motor-bike."

Tamzin rushed to her room, pulled on a pair of shorts and a blue shirt, threw her bedclothes back and ran gaily downstairs. Diccon came towards her in the hall, not looking at her. His face was firmly set, and he was saying "Br-r-r-r" as he came.

Tamzin stooped to plant a kiss on his head as he passed and said, "Hallo, Dicky, darling!"

Diccon paused and turned, regarding her with childish dignity, "NO kiss motor-bike!" he said, and solemnly resumed his tour of the Vicarage ground floor.

"Isn't he SWEET?" Tamzin demanded fervently of her father who was sorting letters in the porch. "Did you hear what he said?"

"You were just as sweet when you were two, and much better tempered. You were about that age when we first came down here."

Tamzin felt surprised at this and said, "Tell me something funny I said when I was two!"

"I can't remember anything."

"Oh, surely Daddy! THINK!"

Mr. Grey thought.

"Well there was once when you first saw a gas works. The gasometer was up and you said, 'Too heavy for me!' You were two-and-a-half."

"DID I, Daddy? How lovely! Tell me some more!"

"Can't! I'm going to feed the chickens. Coming, Diccon Boy?"

Tamzin began to put things on the tray for breakfast. Then she pulled open a dresser drawer and took out a hair brush and comb, two slides and two red ribbons. Mrs. Grey came in, opening letters. "Got your hair things ready? Good!" she said. "Two bills and a catalogue."

"Not so good!" said Tamzin.

Mrs. Grey stuffed the letters in her apron pocket and began undoing Tamzin's plaits. "I see Diccon's been at the salt again," she said, noticing a little white trail by the larder door.

"Has he? Must've been before I came down. Funny how he likes salt so much, isn't it? I believe he really prefers it to sugar. Do you suppose it's very bad for him?"

"Not very, I should think. Might do more harm to forbid it. But I don't encourage him." She twisted a small rubber band on the end of a plait before tying on the ribbon.

"Which slide've you put on that side, Mummy?"

"They look alike to me."

"One's a bit darker brown. I like that one on my RIGHT side."

"This IS the palest," Mrs. Grey said, examining.

"Oh, good!" Tamzin said, with relief.

"I can't see how it matters at all," Mrs. Grey remarked, "since you've a middle parting."

"Oh, I just like them that way," Tamzin said, as if that explained.

Diccon came trotting in ahead of Mr. Grey, caught sight of his salt-trail, reminded himself, and said, "More salt, Boy!" in an announcing kind of voice.

"Ought he to?" Mr. Grey queried, as his son disappeared into the larder.

"He'll grow out of it," Mrs. Grey said, putting away the brush and comb and busying herself with toast.

After breakfast, Tamzin cantered through her holiday jobs of table-clearing, bed-making and wiping-up, before getting out her bicycle and setting forth to meet Rissa at the lifeboat house.

"Thought you'd be along," Old Jim told her, handing her bicycle into the boat. "Yer ma ain't the woman to punish pluck. No more ain't yer Dad the man to despise it."

Tamzin was embarrassed at this personal address and said, "We aren't staying for dinner to-day, Jim. Rissa is booked to take a Dairy pony for shoeing this afternoon, and I've promised to take round parish magazines."

Jim rowed in reflective silence.

"We're only going along to ask after the horse," she added. "Mr. Randall asked us to."

"Did 'e now? Well, I reckon I'll be seein' you most days this summer."

"Oh, I don't know. He only said ' to ask after the horse.'"

Jim had no more to say but looked enigmatic. He always had an air of seeing more in everything than any one else could.

Tamzin was soon at the meeting-place and found Rissa had just arrived.

"I've brought some sugar for the horses," Rissa said, "and two pieces for Carillon."

"I've got carrots," Tamzin said. "They were what Miss Wade gave yesterday. Perhaps sugar's bad for their teeth; they can't clean them like we do."

"I shouldn't think a little matters," Rissa replied, making up her mind to go one better and bring apples next time. Windfalls were cheap just now.

They cycled straight past the Starling's gate without looking that way, in case John should be out in the garden. They were both quite fond of the little chap and wouldn't have dreamed of hurting his feelings about his beloved rabbits, but it did seem to be asking for trouble to catch his eye. Especially as to-day they had only the morning before them.

At the riding stables they found four heads only, over the green half-doors. Carillon's box was empty, the door standing open. For a few moments they stood, shattered by a wave of dismay. Miss Wade, looking up from a broom she was mending in the yard, saw their faces and understood.

"He's doing fine!" she called. "Mr. Randall's taken him back to Tonbridge to be under our own vet. They left early this morning."

Tamzin breathed a loud sigh of relief. "For half a minute I thought he must be dead," she said. "I'm *so* glad he's feeling better."

"Come along in!" Miss Wade said. "I won't be a minute with this broom. Head's loose." The girls climbed over the gate and began patting the horses' heads. "May we give them some sugar?" Rissa asked.

"A little won't hurt," Miss Wade said, "but carrots and apples are best."

Tamzin felt very stable-wise as she broke up her scrubbed carrots, but the horses did seem much more delighted with Rissa's sugar-lumps.

"Are you going to manage all right now, with only four horses and ponies?" Rissa asked, as Miss Wade walked across to them.

"Oh, we shan't have to. We have several at Tonbridge, you know, and Mr. Randall will bring one back. Unless he changes his mind it will be a very showy skewbald called Timpani."

"A skewbald! How lovely!" Tamzin exclaimed. "But what a funny name. Why not Timothy?"

"It means 'drums,'" explained Rissa, who was learning music. "I think it's a perfect name for a horse, when you think of galloping hoofs."

"Oh, yes, when you know what it means, it IS!" Tamzin agreed.

Miss Wade said:

"He goes with the other musical horses. Mr. Randall is very fond of music and likes musical names. Had you noticed?"

"Well, there's Allegro," Rissa said, thinking. "It means 'swiftly and lightly,' doesn't it?"

"Something like that," Miss Wade replied. "And Carillon, of course; a peal of bells. And in Tonbridge

Splashing buckets of water.

there are Madrigal and Minstrel, as well as the skewbald, Timpani."

"I think it's rather a good idea," Tamzin said, "and there must be such an endless choice. How funny!" she added, "I thought yesterday that if I ever have a pony I might call it Woodwind, and that's a musical name, too!"

Miss Wade said, "I have to carry water before my pupil comes. Like to help?"

"Oh, YES! May we?"

"Come along then. Buckets are in the saddle-room. Water's our bugbear here; we have to fetch it from Murphy's."

The saddle-room was orderly and smelt of clean leather, saddle-soap and hay. Bridles hung limply round the walls, six saddles were ranged on a long trestle saddle-horse, and four trusses of hay stood stacked in a corner beside a large iron corn-bin. On a wooden bench were two tins of saddle-soap, a tin of metal-polish and a group of small sponges and folded rubbers.

Miss Wade took down a wooden yoke from the wall, and hung a couple of buckets on the chains. "You two can carry a bucket between you," she said, handing one from under the bench.

"Donkey's gone," Rissa said, as they clanked into Murphy's field.

"Yes. Mr. Murphy was very nice about it, and offered himself to move the donkey to a further field. Most horses are frightened of donkeys, you know."

"And pigs, too," Tamzin put in. "Farmer Merrow's Tinkle HATES their pigs."

As they returned with slopping pails Miss Wade said, "I have a Miss Wilkins coming at ten for an hour on Allegro. I'm taking Ballerina, and if you two like you can come with us on the ponies. They aren't booked till three o'clock, and the exercise will do them good."

"You mean, RIDE them?" said Tamzin, weakly.

"Yes, of course! Why not? I had orders from the Boss to be sure you got some riding. You're heroines, you know! Don't forget that," she twinkled at them, amused at their astonishment. "Carillon is a very valuable horse, and our still having him is quite probably entirely due to you. So we're saying Thank you with the freedom of the stables."

"Oh, I s-*say*!" stuttered Rissa. Tamzin was utterly speechless.

Miss Wade laughed. "Oh, come! It's such a LITTLE thing compared with what you did for Carillon."

They lowered the heavy buckets to the saddle-room floor, and Tamzin straightened up and found her voice. "This is his-hisTORIC!" she announced, but Miss Wade, who thought their modesty delicious, only laughed again.

"Come and saddle up your ponies!" she said.

The girls floated on air. Saddling up was pure delight; the tackle was softer and finer than anything they had handled before. Farmer Merrow never touched his bits of leather with anything, and the Dairy ponies had only their blinker-bridles and no saddles at all.

Miss Wilkins arrived in a small green car, and was assisted to mount the white-faced Allegro. Miss Wade felt the ponies' girths, lowered Rissa's leathers a couple of holes for her long legs, and swung up into Ballerina's saddle. The procession filed out of the yard; Tamzin, nearly bursting with corked-up excitement, on the little bay Sea Pie, and Rissa, trying

to look as if she did this every day, on the dapple-
grey Cobweb, who was nearly fourteen hands and
inclined to be over-keen for a learner.

Down the grass track they went at a decorous
walk, across the road and through the Cut in the
dunes, where Ballerina broke into a school-trot.
The girls shortened rein, squeezed with their calves
and followed after, with Allegro dancing up behind.
Miss Wade glanced over her shoulder and said,
"Don't hold him too tight," to Miss Wilkins who
was hanging on to her reins. They came out on the
famous stretch of hard yellow sand where Derby
horses had been trained, and trotted down to the sea.

The two Hillocks ponies were a revelation to
Tamzin and Rissa, accustomed as they were to the
grudging responses of the ageing Tinkle and the
butcher-boy trot of the two ponies from the Dunsford Dairy. At first they both fell into the mistake
of making their "aids" too strong. A leg-squeeze
meant to signal "walk a little faster" producing a
sudden canter, and a pull on the reins meant to
indicate "no, I meant trot" landing them at a total
standstill. Soon they discovered that these well-
schooled ponies responded to a touch, almost indeed,
to a thought. Riding, for the first time in their lives,
on well-bred, carefully trained ponies, they felt like
creatures in a new element, almost as if they had
suddenly found they could fly.

They pulled up at the edge of the water and Miss
Wade said, "Shall we let them bathe their legs?
They like it, and it's good for them."

They followed through the little waves of the
creeping tide and stood knee-deep. The horses
lowered their heads and blew curiously at the swaying
water, knowing it was salt, and not nice.

"We thought of taking them in for a swim, one day. No saddles, of course, and we'd have to wear swim-suits. Would you like that?"

"Oh, YES!" Tamzin said, and Rissa said, "Can they swim?"

"All horses can," Miss Wade replied. "In fact I believe most animals can if they are put to it; even cats!" Then, "What about a canter? This shore is perfect for it."

"Rather, if you think I can!" said Miss Wilkins, cheerfully, and Miss Wade smiled and said, "You'll be all right if you keep a light rein on her. She's snaffle-mouthed." She turned to the two girls. "The same applies to you! But I've noticed you've been finding that out for yourselves. Cobweb is a bit keen, Rissa, but he's all right if you're light with your legs."

They splashed slowly out of the sea and turned along the tide-mark, Ballerina setting the pace at a collected canter, with Allegro at her side. The girls followed, Tamzin still floating in a dream of bliss, but Rissa having to apply all her skill and intelligence to the proper control of the excitable little grey.

They cantered gloriously along the foam-flecked margin of the tide, the wind in their hair and sea-spray in their faces.

"This—is—SMASHING!" Tamzin said in bursts, her eyes shining and thick plaits bouncing.

"Ought to be riding THIS one," Rissa said, and added, "But it IS marvellous—after Tinkle!"

Miss Wade, busy with her pupil whose hands were inclined to be heavy, spared an intermittent glance towards the girls and a cautionary reminder to Rissa about Cobweb's distaste for heels.

Approaching a very fat woman with an ice-cream barrow even the sensible little Sea Pie was more than shaken when the fat one mounted a stout box and began swinging a heavy brass hand-bell with hearty determination. It was altogether the last straw for Cobweb, who thought the sudden racket absolutely frightful and a menace. He reared, whirled round and set off for home as fast as he could lay legs to ground.

No one was more astonished than Rissa to find herself still in the saddle after this remarkable performance, with no worse calamity than a flying stirrup. This she blindly fumbled for and found as she careered on her abandoned way, scattering beach-parties, strollers, nursemaids and children as she went.

Not being versed in the art of controlling a runaway horse, she leaned back and pulled steadily on the reins with all her strength. And consequently, she did not have any effect at all on the headlong rush until it was abruptly terminated by Cobweb himself, at his own stable door, landing Rissa rudely on his neck with an ungraceful wallop. She slithered to the ground still holding the reins, led him into his box, shut the door and leaned weakly against it.

"Trollop!" she said to him, disgustedly, and set about relieving him of his leather.

The other three arrived back to find her completely recovered and rubbing Cobweb down. He was very hot and sweating, but obviously beginning to feel rather ashamed of himself.

"Well, you look all right, the pair of you!" Miss Wade said in a relieved sort of voice.

"I am anyway, and I think he is," Rissa said. "I just *couldn't* stop him. My fault, I don't doubt, but

He reared and whirled round.

the Merrow's Tinkle doesn't really fit one for this sort of thing."

"I think you were wonderful to stick ON," Miss Wilkins said, from Allegro's box. "I'm sure I shouldn't have!"

"The first bit was the worst," Rissa said, "when he reared and swerved. For the rest I just sat there, but I was of no account whatever to HIM."

"He never has run away before," Miss Wade remarked, coming out with Ballerina's saddle, "But that bell was an earful for a nervous little horse. Can you credit any one being so far-gone as to ring the thing just *then*? What that woman needs is sending a couple of miles on a nappy four-year-old. That'd show her."

Tamzin, burdened under Sea Pie's tackle, nearly collapsed utterly at the comical vision this evoked in her mind.

Miss Wilkins departed noisily in her small green car, and the trio processed to the saddle-room.

"No need to clean any tack now; only the bits. All the horses will be out again, some of them twice, before sunset," Miss Wade told them, as she sorted windfalls in a box. "Have some! They're not all bruised," she said.

They sat casually on an upturned box and trusses of hay, crunching Beauties of Bath and discussing runaway horses till Westling church clock sent the girls flying for their bicycles and home.

CHAPTER FIVE

ARRIVING at Hillocks Stables soon after breakfast the next morning, the girls were instantly made aware of the newcomer. His brown and white face stood out in startling contrast to the more everyday faces of the other four horses. He looked an absolute clown, with one ear white and one brown and a small white muzzle at the end of a long brown face.

Mr. Randall was with him in his box, a rubber in his hand. Hearing the gate he looked up and called, "Come and have a look at the patchwork quilt!"

The girls walked across and leaned over the door, a little shyly.

"I LOVE skewbalds!" Tamzin said.

"I have a weakness for them, myself," Mr. Randall agreed. "And this one has rather exceptionally showy markings, don't you think?"

He was certainly most attractively marked, with milk-white mane and tail against brown neck and quarters, his body half white with continents of rich brown reaching to his knees and hocks, and four white stockings running down to clean pink hooves.

"He's so beautiful he might have been designed," Rissa said.

"And he's as quiet as a lamb," Mr. Randall remarked. "You could put a toddler on him, for all that he's the finest jumper I've got. I'll show you his rosettes one day. Meanwhile, I've got something for you in the saddle-room. Come along!"

He shut the green door and led the way round the stables. In the saddle-room, Miss Wade looked

up from the bench where she was polishing stirrup-
irons and smiled "Good-morning!"

Mr. Randall pulled open a drawer and took out
two light hunting-crops complete with thongs.

"A small token," he said, "with Carillon's heart-
felt gratitude!" He smiled, half-mocking, half-
serious, handing the crops. The girls took them
with bewildered thanks, and Rissa added, flushing,
"You needn't have. Just coming here and riding was
much more than enough reward."

"This isn't a reward," Mr. Randall said. "It's a
sort of solid Thank you."

Tamzin turned her crop lovingly in her hands,
staring at its details. "There's something written!"
she said, looking closer, and read the almost micro-
scopic words, " In grateful appreciation from Guy
Randall and Carillon.'"

"We've got a child coming this morning to ride
Sea Pie, but Rissa can have Cobweb and you, Tamzin,
can ride the skewbald," Mr. Randall said, brushing
aside the matter of the crops and taking down
bridles. "You'll find him a bit big for real comfort,
but his manners are quite perfect."

Miss Wade helped them saddle up, and said she
hoped they'd brought their swim-suits because it
looked like being a good day for swimming the
horses. The girls said they had, and had also brought
sandwiches for dinner; and Tamzin remarked with
decision that they really ought to have jodhpurs
now they had crops, because you can't very well
carry a crop in shorts, and as Rissa was best at
explaining, perhaps she had better come Westling
way home and help her with HER explaining, too.

Rissa said "All right," by which time the horses
were saddled and every one was only waiting for

the child, who was called Roy Hay, and his aunt, a Miss Polkinghorne, who was to ride Allegro side-saddle.

They arrived five minutes late in a navy-blue Chrysler, and the girls at once decided that they didn't care for the side-saddle habit, though it was certainly extremely smart. Much too hot for August, any way.

Miss Wade was to escort the party on Ballerina while Mr. Randall did some chaff-cutting and water-carrying.

Tamzin had to have a leg-up because Timpani was over sixteen hands, and Miss Wade held Allegro for Miss Polkinghorne to mount. Rissa and the boy scrambled up unaided, and they all filed through the gate.

They took an inland track across marshy fields stocked with black-nosed sheep, and Tamzin discovered what a delightful action a big horse has, after having only ridden ponies before, though the skewbald was much too big for her to be able to use her legs properly.

They cantered several times on the short-cropped grass, and Rissa found she was now much better able to control the lively grey, and could give an eye now and then to the riding of the Hay-Polking-horne couple.

Roy was probably not more than seven, but had the makings of a good rider. He sat well down in his saddle and did not haul on his pony's mouth. Not that any one would ever feel the need to with Sea Pie, who was most responsive.

Miss Polkinghorne was so polished in her style that she almost seemed artificial.

Joan Wade dealt with gates efficiently and

smoothly, telling the girls that this was where
their crops would come in most useful. They
circled towards the dunes, came through a second
cut further along the shore and cantered homewards
along the hard, ribbed sand. Rissa had some difficulty
in keeping Cobweb collected at this point, but got
along pretty well and was able to relax a little on
the last half-mile, when every one was walking
in order to bring the horses home cool.

Arriving at the stables, the horses were put in
their boxes and the saddles removed.

"We'll leave the bridles on while we change,"
Miss Wade said. "The horses aren't hot, but we'll
walk them to the sea, to make sure."

Miss Polkinghorne said, "Monday at two, then,"
and followed her nephew into the navy-blue
Chrysler. In the saddle-room, Mr. Randall took a
pair of black swimming-trunks from the bench
drawer and went off to an empty box. The girls
and Miss Wade changed on trusses of hay and the
corn-bin, and discussed side-saddle riding. Tamzin
said there *was* something very graceful about it, but
she didn't like the habit. Rissa said it couldn't be
half so comfortable for a horse as the cross-saddle,
and Miss Wade said you certainly needed to be expert
to ride a horse properly side-saddle as it was more
difficult to balance the weight, and in any case, even
if the weight WAS central, it was almost impossible
to get it far enough forward. She said Miss Polkinghorne was accustomed to hunt side-saddle with the
Bicester, and was pretty good. She was on holiday
down here with her nephew's family and would
come to Hillock's fairly often during August.

They gathered in the stable-yard, feeling a little
ridiculous, like people suddenly finding themselves

Tamzin said there was something graceful about it.

in pyjamas in the street. Mr. Randall, looking hard and brown in his absurd black trunks, said he proposed riding Ballerina and leading Allegro. Which left Joan Wade with Timpani and the girls with the two ponies. Whereupon Rissa said she thought she'd be much safer on Timpani than on Cobweb, but was told she would have a much better grip on the smaller animal, and this was vital on a wet, bare back.

Mr. Randall swung them all up on their astonished mounts and apparently flew on to the white mare's back, himself.

"Reminds me of the Dairy ponies," Tamzin said, as they set forth.

"I don't see *any* resemblance!" Rissa said, quite shocked.

"Oh, I just meant the riding without saddles," Tamzin explained.

Mr. Randall said none of the horses had been actually swum before, but most horses took happily to the water and they were likely to have an uneventful time of it.

They filed through the Cut and down the sands to the sea, which was rather far out for their purpose. They had to wade the horses quite a distance before the water reached their middles. It was at this depth that the gentle Timpani suddenly surprised every one by declining to go a single step further. He was in no way disagreeable about it but just said NO. And nothing Miss Wade did had the slightest effect on his attitude towards the matter. The others went calmly on as if they had been swimming every day for years. Even Cobweb wallowed placidly forward in water now more than half-way up his flanks. Ballerina was frankly enjoying herself, pushing at the water with her muzzle and snorting playfully into oncoming ripples, with Allegro plunging boatlike at her side.

The ponies, being smaller, were swimming first, only their heads showing above the rippled water. The girls were keeping balanced with a twist of mane, and once Tamzin was washed right off Sea Pie's back but hauled herself easily back again with her handhold as anchor.

"Don't they LURCH!" she said to Rissa, who was finding Cobweb more manageable in the water than he had ever been on land.

Tamzin laughed, "Yes! The action is quite different from anything they do on land."

"Turn now!" Mr. Randall called. "Mustn't overdo it, first time!"

Swinging round they were met by the skewbald, who had suddenly decided this might be worth trying after all. He looked more like a circus turn than ever, prancing in the sea with Joan Wade aloft in a slinky striped swim-suit. Coming out was tricky; the horses plunged as they began to find their feet, and there was practically no grip on their smooth streaming backs. Rissa found herself being pulled on to Cobweb's neck but managed to slither back. The horses were keen to gallop, coming on to firm sand from the uncertain sea, and Mr. Randall said they'd most likely be all right if they headed straight for the dunes where the steep, soft sandhills would help pull them up.

They loosened rein, expecting the worst, but found this wild wet gallop quite the most exhilerating thing they had ever done. It was not difficult to keep mounted, but they couldn't have pulled up if Niagara had opened up before them. They thundered on, laughing at the tops of their voices and gaily putting all their trust in the high dunes ahead. They could hear Mr. Randall's two horses, well in control and cantering up behind. Timpani was out of earshot, probably still in the sea.

The ponies raced joyously to the foot of the dunes and, obeying the girls' hopeful aids, charged

The horses plunged.

valiantly at the steep soft bank. Their small hoofs sank deeply into the shifting surface, and their shoulder muscles hardened. Before they were half-way up they were heavily trotting, and at the top of the dune they walked to a breathless stop, their wet sides heaving under the girl's bare legs.

Mr. Randall was walking his horses through the Cut, and Timpani just cantering up from the sea. The girls waved from their hilltop, and were

signalled on down the other side where they filed
along a footpath leading into the Cut. Timpani
jogged up to join them, and they walked homewards
in a little veil of steam from sun-drying horses and
riders.

Mr. Randall was saying what about the Gymkhana, and Rissa replied that the last time they'd
discussed it they had decided to ask Farmer Merrow
if they could ride Tinkle in some of the simpler
events, like Musical Chairs and Bending. But they
didn't think they'd be able to get in much practice;
Farmer Merrow could be difficult. Mr. Randall
said how about riding Sea Pie and Cobweb? It was
always good business for a riding school to have
ponies in a gymkhana, so they needn't bother about
being grateful.

This suggestion was most enthusiastically received
until Tamzin suddenly said, "We've never jumped.
We couldn't do any of the jumping classes."

Mr. Randall said why worry about that? He and
Miss Wade were both jumping, so the ponies could
very well concentrate on non-jumping classes.
"Nevertheless," he added, "it would be a good idea
to put up some little jumps one day and give you
both some schooling over them. Cobweb partic-
ularly is a first-rate jumper, and Sea Pie is pretty
good."

Rissa said it was a smashing idea, and Tamzin said
when could they begin?

"To-day's Saturday, and so we're booked right
up," Mr. Randall said. "And to-morrow's about as
busy. Say Monday?"

"Yes, Monday's good for both of us. We go to
church on Sunday mornings, anyhow." They
reached the stable-yard and clattered in.

"Horses are nearly dry," Miss Wade remarked, slipping off Timpani's now sticky back.

"Want a rub over, though," Mr. Randall said from Allegro's box.

"Can we do the ponies?" Rissa asked, coming into the open with Cobweb's bridle.

"Yes, and gladly, only rub yourselves down and dress first. A wisp of hay'll clean your feet a bit, but be sure not to put it back with the fresh!"

They pattered to the saddle-room and peeled off their clammy swim-suits. Joan Wade, towelling briskly, said they might manage to put up some poles and practise bending too, on Monday. They scambled into their clothes, rubbed their feet, slipped on their shoes and went to the horses, armed with hay-wisps for rubbing.

"Rub good and thoroughly, especially round the ears and armpits," Mr. Randall called, and the girls got down to it vigorously. After the rubbing they helped to feed the eager horses who "nickered" softly over their half-doors at the sound of the corn-bin lid creaking back. Miss Wade measured out the feed of one third oats, one third bran and one third chaff, and saying "Sea Pie," or "Timpani," or "Allegro," handed out horses' dinners in sieves. Rissa, taking Cobweb's ration, met Mr. Randall coming from rubbing Ballerina.

"You girls got sandwiches?" he asked. "Well, make yourselves comfortable in the saddle-room if you like. Miss Wade and I feed at our boarding house. We'll be gone about an hour. We're booked right up for this afternoon and evening, allowing for rests all round, so you won't be able to get in any more riding to-day. But come and go as you like. We're glad to see you any time."

He went on round the sheds for the white mare's feed.

In the saddle-room, Miss Wade and Tamzin were discussing names, and Miss Wade was saying she knew some people called Sidebottom who pronounced it Siddybotoam. Rissa came in with the empty sieve and laughed. "How crazy!" she said. "Like those people we once met called Enchickwistle!"

They picked up damp towels and swim-suits and draped them over the fence outside the door. "Let's eat in the sun by the wall here," Tamzin said, rummaging in her bicycle-bag for lunch packets. They stretched their legs and leaned contentedly against the sun-warmed wall of the saddle-room.

"Think of school after this!" Tamzin murmured, undoing paper.

"DON'T think of it!" Rissa returned, looking to see what Tamzin had got. "Your mother does give you the most scrummy lunches!" she said, noticing two bananas, a cold baked potato split and filled with butter, a tomato and some crisp lettuce-leaves in a grease-proof bag. There were sandwiches and a piece of cake besides.

"Well, you've got sausages," Tamzin pointed out, "and I hardly ever get THEM."

"They're all Mummy ever thinks of," Rissa deplored. "Swop for a banana?"

"M-m-m!" Tamzin said, handing one. She doted on cold sausage.

"Funny, how one always wants what one hasn't got," Rissa remarked, munching.

"I don't," Tamzin said. "I wouldn't swop lives with any one else at Dunsford High School just this minute. Can't imagine being any happier than I am."

"And you were just saying 'think of school!'" Rissa said.

"Drat you! Reminding me! But honestly it doesn't bear thinking about. I mean school and winter, and taking Dairy ponies to the forge on Saturday mornings. . . ."

"M'm. After holidays and summer and all THIS." Rissa waved an expressive arm.

They relapsed into a thoughful, digesting sort of silence, and then Rissa said heartily, "Well, there's always next summer!"

Tamzin gave her a withering look and began on her banana.

CHAPTER SIX

CYCLING PRECARIOUSLY through the half-open Vicarage gate that afternoon, they narrowly missed Diccon who jumped out of the tamarisks beside the path and yelled, "Wissa, Wissa! Tamsie, Tamsie! Boy bykle wide, P'EASE!"

The girls swerved into the pergola-roses and fell off. Diccon bounced across the path and embraced his sister where she sat, beneath the roses. "Tamsie all-fall-down! Boy kissit better!" he remarked with satisfaction.

Rissa crawled muddily from under her bicycle. "He does sound PLEASED when one crashes, somehow, even though he hands out kisses," she commented, straightening her handlebars. "Dicky come and have a ride?" she offered, patting her saddle. He came stoutly up to her and presented his back to be lifted.

"You know Mummy doesn't really like people calling him "'Dicky,'" Tamzin reproved.

"Oh well, I can't seem to help it sometimes. He's such a lamb!" Rissa excused. "And anyway, you do it yourself." She wheeled the grubby-faced lamb round the house, with Tamzin pedal-scooting ahead. Mrs. Grey smiled at them through the kitchen window as they passed, and they dumped their cycles in the shed, gathered up Diccon and went in.

"Scones!" Tamzin said, nose up.

"Hot ones, too!" Rissa added.

"Yes, with strawberry jam. Hurry up and wash

hands! You're staying, aren't you, Rissa?" Mrs. Grey said, putting tea in the pot.

"May I? Oh, thanks!"

They dashed upstairs, Tamzin panting, "Don't forget the jodhs. We MUST, for the gymkhana. Think of shorts in the show-ring!"

"Do your own explaining," Rissa said firmly, grabbing soap, "but I'll back you up."

In the drawing-room they found the family already gathered. Mr. Grey, who was cutting bread-and-butter into little squares for Diccon, looked up and smiled in his rather absent way and began topping the squares with tiny blobs of honey. He put them before Diccon on the farm-yard table mat, and drew the cup of milk-cocoa a little further from exploring hands. The girls sat down and looked hungrily over the table.

"Scones and honey?" Mrs. Grey suggested. "It's clover honey, and rather good."

They devoured scones and honey.

"Had a good time?" Mrs. Grey said, handing tea.

"M-m! Rather! We swam the horses."

"SWAM the horses?" Mr. Grey looked perplexed.

"Yes, in the sea. It's good for them, and they like it. We wore swim-suits and no saddles."

"She means the horses wore no saddles," Rissa explained, through clover honey.

"No saddles!" Diccon echoed dreamily, making a train with his squares of bread-and-butter.

"He doesn't know what it means!" Tamzin said. "And LOOK what he's doing with his tea!"

"Train, Boy," Diccon said, sweetly, "Engine too !" He pointed to one sticky morsel balanced fantastically on another.

"He never eats it when he starts making trains of it," Mr. Grey complained to his wife.

"Give him a fork to prod them up with," she suggested, and Diccon, approving this idea, prodded them up and through a bursting mouth said, "Chocky drink, Boy!"

The meal progressed, and Tamzin despairingly pedalled Rissa's feet under the table and said, "Jodhs!" in a sibilant whisper. Rissa took no notice whatever and went on staring out of the window. They had got to the fruit cake, and Diccon was already saying "Bib off!" and loosing interest in the ruins of the spread.

Finding no further demands round the table for food, Mrs. Grey rose and went to her son. She removed his bib, having first wiped his mouth with it, and lifted him down.

"Sank you much," Diccon said politely, and then, "'Mulsion, Boy!"

"Does he need emulsion in the summer?" Mr. Grey inquired, pushing in his chair.

"Not really," his wife replied, unscrewing the bottle, "but he likes it."

Diccon took the spoonful with blissfully closed eyes, opened them suddenly and said, "More!"

Mrs. Grey gave him a half a teaspoonful, and Mr. Grey said, "He'll be sick!" and went to his study to prepare his sermons for the morrow.

"Find sugar-sweetie tin," Diccon announced, and trotted out.

Mrs. Grey said, "There's something in your room for you, Tamzin. Go and see if you can find it while I clear the table."

The girls dashed upstairs, jodhpurs momentarily

forgotten. They burst into the attic bedroom and glanced swiftly around it.

"There it is!" Rissa said, pointing.

They rushed across to Tamzin's bed and stood on it so as to get a better view of a picture hanging at the head.

"Bad for the springs!" Rissa said, and they flopped to their knees on the pillow. It was a fairly large coloured print of three horses' heads at a manger full of hay and roots. There were two white heads and one black and there was a pigeon on the manger's brim.

"Oh, Tam, how absolutely gorgeous! You do get the loveliest things!"

"Yes, it is. But I don't. What about your bicycle? Three-speed and a pump and shiny rims. And mine was ten-and-six in a junk shop."

"Well, that's not quite the same . . ." Rissa began, and turned at the puffing sound of Diccon ascending the stairs. Between each puff was a whacking bang; the sweetie tin coming up too. Mrs. Grey was behind him.

"Barley sugars!" Rissa said, opening the tin.

"Mummy DARLING," Tamzin said, pulling her down on the bed, "where DID you get it?"

"Well, you know my Van Huysum: 'Flowers in a Vase?'"

"Yes. The one with a snail and hollyhocks that's in your room?"

"That WAS in my room! These horses were underneath it. I had them over my bed when I was ten, and long afterwards, too. In fact, till after you were born. Then one day your Aunt Gabrielle came to visit us, and when she saw the horses she teased me a lot about them and said they 'weren't good Art,'

and 'Fancy still having them.' She brought the
Van Huysum print on her next visit and persuaded
me to have it up instead. But I kept the three horses
where they were, only behind the new print!"

"Mummy! Fancy letting yourself be bullied like
that!"

"I didn't. I rather thought she might be right,
and the Van Huysum IS very lovely. I shall have it
up again when I can find a frame to fit it."

"Yes, I liked it too," Rissa said. "It looked as if
the sun were shining on it, and I liked the snail."

"But it wasn't beautiful enough to hide these
darling horses all those years!" Tamzin said. "Are
they REALLY bad art, Mummy?"

"No, I don't think so. They may not be in the
same flight as 'Flowers in a Vase,' artistically speaking, but I think they're genuinely good. And they
were painted by a man who used to drive a hansom
for a living! I forget his name. . . ."

They turned and trailed downstairs, Mrs. Grey
carrying Diccon. He had a barley sugar in each
cheek.

"I shall look at them every night last thing, and
every morning first thing," Tamzin said, "and they
shall all have names. The black will be Black
Barbary, but I shall have to think about the others."

"You've got THREE white horses in your room
now," Rissa said, "with the Lucy Kemp-Welsh
galloping horse you had for Christmas; he's a
beauty, too. Wild, I should think. And I've *still*
got only my nursery: 'Lambkins!'"

"Poor old Rissa!" Tamzin said with genuine
feeling. How much better to be the daughter of a
poor country clergyman and have an exciting bedroom (even if the furniture WAS stained deal), than

to be the child of a 'comfortable' wood-merchant and have to sleep in a pink and grey room with furniture that showed marks, and 'Lambkins.'

"Shall we wash-up?" Tamzin offered, arriving at the ground floor.

"That's very nice of you!" Mrs. Grey said. "Then I can take Diccon down to feed the chickens for Daddy. He's busy with his sermons."

"We'll do that too!" Tamzin called, on her way to the scullery and bursting with warm gratitude.

Over the wiping-up Rissa said, "Well, what about your jodhs *now*?"

"Couldn't possibly after the picture. They'll have to wait a bit."

They left everything as tidy as they could, and Tamzin remembered to wipe the splashes off the draining-board. Then they went down to feed the chickens, and Tamzin showed Rissa her own special pullet who was called Maia and was a cuckoo-coloured bird which laid very dark brown eggs, because she was a Marans fowl and they all laid eggs like that.

"Daddy says he'll have a stitting of Marans in the spring, now Maia's been so successful. She was just an experiment, you see."

"We haven't shown them our crops!" Rissa suddenly said, from the depths of a nesting-box.

"No, so we haven't! And they're still in our bicycle saddle-bags! How many eggs? Is there a very dark one?"

"Four, and no dark one. They're all sort of middling—see?" Rissa backed out of the hen-house two eggs in each hand.

They went round by the cycle shed and took their crops from the saddle-bags. Mrs. Grey was weeding the rose beds into Diccon's little wheelbarrow, and Diccon was wheeling the weeds to the compost heap with happy industry.

"Look, Mummy!" Tamzin ran, holding out the little crop. "And Rissa's got one, too."

"My dears, but how lovely! Where did they come from?"

"It says on them. Look, there."

Mrs. Grey read, then looked up, "How very nice of him! We must show these to Daddy, sermons or no. Come along now, you young heroines!"

"You're teasing!"

"Of course I am! It's good for you."

They arrived at the study door, knocked and went in.

"Anything the matter?" Mr. Grey glanced up anxiously at this unheard-of family intrusion.

"We want to show you these, Richard, before Rissa has to go."

"Bless my soul! What next? Where did you get 'em?"

Mrs. Grey pointed to the tiny inscriptions, and her husband adjusted his reading-glasses. "H'm! Horse very valuable?"

"Miss Wade said so," Tamzin told him, doubtful of his attitude. She often found it difficult to know whether he was pleased or angry or neither.

"Well, from all I hear you deserved 'em, you young rascals!" He handed them back, smiling broadly. "Now get along! I'm having frightful trouble with Absalom. Your mother said he was an awkward subject for a sermon, and she was right."

Tamzin threw her arms round him and gave him a loud kiss, dislodging his glasses and scattering sermon-papers which Diccon at once picked up, scrutinised, and sat down with, saying in a piercing squeak, "Train! See train! Engine too; see wheels!" He dabbed the written lines delightedly with a muddy finger.

"He thinks the writing's trains!" Rissa said. "Isn't he SWEET?"

Mrs. Grey salvaged the sermon and put it back on her husband's desk, smoothing the creases with her fingers.

"At least we can be thankful that they don't catch horses every day," the Vicar said, settling his glasses and resuming his trouble with Absalom.

"I'll come with you to the wishing gate," Tamzin was saying, going out of the door with her friend, "because we haven't wished since Thursday."

Sitting in the Vicarage pew all by herself the next morning, Tamzin hadn't the remotest idea what her father was saying about Absalom. Her head was like the middle of a roundabout, ringed dizzily with revolving jodhpurs, ponies, riding-crops, bending-poles and rabbits.

The August sun shone dustily down on her through the high leaded window above the Vicarage pew. Her face, so rapt and quiet that even her father put it down to interest in his sermon, was lightly tanned and flushed like a warm, ripe apricot.

However, Mr. Grey was not the only person in the church who noticed Tamzin's guilty start when the congregation rose to its squeaky feet for *Now to God the Father*. Old Jim the ferryman, sitting in the pew behind as he had done nearly every Sunday morning for the past forty years, had been studying her through lowered bushy eyebrows.

Tamzin joined hastily in the final hymn, cheered

Sitting in the Vicarage pew all by herself.

by thoughts of approaching air and sunshine, of roast beef and browned potatoes for dinner (yes, even on an August Sunday. The tradition was like wash-day on Monday; immovable), and of Diccon's eager welcome when he saw her coming home. She hurried out in the forefront of the departing congregation saying, "Good-morning, Mrs. Briggs! Lovely day, Mr. Downey!" and "How do you do, Miss Siddle?" as she overtook the flock.

She took the short-cut home behind the school, and over the Vicarage garden wall. Mrs. Grey was laying the dinner table with Diccon's precarious help, as Tamzin burst joyfully into the dining-room swinging her hat.

"Mummy! Diccon, DARLING!" She whirled round the table and hugged them both in an overflow of spirits.

"Was the congregation good?" Mrs. Grey inquired, through the edge of the straw brim.

"Quite," said Tamzin vaguely. "What's for pudding? Plum tart? Goody! And cream? Oh, my!"

"And someone rang you up; a Mr. Randall," her mother said, with a provocative smile.

"Mr. Randall? Telephoned ME? Oh, Mummy, what about? Tell me quick, or I'll pop!"

"He said they were so booked up for this afternoon that he'd decided not to ride, in order to leave an extra horse. And that he thought he'd run up to Tonbridge to see Carillon."

"Oh, was that all?" Tamzin sounded just a little disappointed.

"And he said perhaps you and Rissa might like to go too. You could pick her up in Dunsford on your way."

"Oh, MUMMY!"

"You're to be at the lifeboat house at half-past two, and with a warm coat because it's an open car."

"Oh, MUMMY!"

"What's the matter? Aren't you pleased?"

"Well, yes, in a way, but it's dreadful, because when we were at Merrow's last Sunday we promised we'd be there to-day to fetch Tinkle for them to go to tea with the married daughter. What rotten luck!"

"Well, look, I don't think you really need worry. Diccon and I can go that way for our walk this afternoon and explain. In any case I wanted to go before long to ask Mr. Merrow about the sheaves for the harvest festival. He gets it all threshed if we don't remind him early."

"Oh, WOULD you? Oh, how lovely! Does Rissa know?"

"You can ring her now, while I dish up. I can hear Daddy at the gate. Diccon, go and meet Daddy in the garden?"

The two children whisked through the door like a March breeze, and Mrs. Grey walked kitchenwards to assemble the traditional dinner.

At the ferry that afternoon Old Jim gave Tamzin a shrewd look. "Yer pa," he began, "'e do 'ave a way er seein' fifty sides to a simple question. Now take this 'ere Absalom chap. Danged if I know yet whether 'e were fer 'im or agin 'im. Now what would YOU say, Miss Tamzin?"

Tamzin opened her mouth, shut it again and looked narrowly at Jim. "Well, to be absolutely honest, Jim, I've no idea at all," she said.

CHAPTER SEVEN

MONDAY MORNING saw the girls at the stables before ten. Mr. Randall was already out with a holiday couple who had never ridden in their lives before, and was not expected back till half-past ten.

"Just leaves us nice time to get some poles in for bending," Miss Wade said. "We ought to manage all right in this sandy soil. We borrowed some fairly good poles from Mr. Murphy; they're in the corner of the paddock." She picked up a wooden mallet and said, "Come along and we'll see what we can make of it."

They climbed over the fence and walked to the little stack of chestnut poles. "You've put some jumps up!" Rissa said.

"Yes, just three little ones. We might improve on them in a day or two, but we shan't do much in that line down here. Did you see the jumping paddock at Tonbridge?"

"Oh yes, it's super! So many different kinds of jumps, and even a jumping-lane and an in-and-out."

"Yes, we spent a long time improving that jumping paddock. But tell me about Carillon. What did you think of him?"

"Oh, he was a pet!" Rissa said. "He nuzzled just as if he remembered us."

"But his legs were awfully bruised and swollen," Tamzin said, picking up poles, "And the vet thinks his show-jumping's over, at least. Isn't it dreadfully sad? He's such a lovely horse."

Miss Wade set down her poles and studied the

lay-out of the field. "Yes, it does seem a pity. But he's likely to be perfectly all right for hacking, and of course he MAY even be able to hunt and jump again. It's rather early to begin getting down-hearted." She set up her pole. "Can you hold this steady while I knock it in, Rissa?"

Tamzin stooped for a second pole and held it ready. "We loved the darling little strawberry roan," she said, watching the swinging mallet. "She's only about twelve hands, isn't she?"

"Oh, Midge? She's eleven-two. She's quite the pet of the stables. Sometimes she takes a child hunting, and as often as not the child is whisked off home in a car after a couple of hours or so, but no one ever thinks of taking Midge home. We just run her stirrups up, fix the reins under the leathers and tell her to go home. She sets off all by herself, keeping to the proper side of the road and trotting along as sensible as you like!"

"What a darling she must be!" Tamzin said. "And what happens when she gets home?"

"She whinnies outside the gate till someone comes and lets her in. And once when no one heard her she went right round to the garden gate, pushed it open, trotted up to the house and whinnied at the front door till Mr. Randall's housekeeper came and took her down to her box."

Rissa said, "She must be most awfully intelligent."

Joan Wade took a pole from Tamzin and surveyed the row she had already fixed. "They look straight enough, don't you think?" she said, shutting one eye.

"Beautiful!" Rissa agreed, and they bent to it again.

"Doesn't any one ever think she's a runaway and stop her?" Tamzin asked.

"No, everyone knows her for miles around. She used to trot like that just ahead of us before we ever sent her alone, so people got used to it gradually, I suppose. And the stables are well outside the town and busy traffic."

The row of poles grew longer and with the last one Miss Wade straightened up, squinted along the line and said, "I think that will do. Come along and get your ponies ready."

They were mounted and in the field before Mr. Randall had seen his holiday couple safely down the track on their bicycles, and joined the bending party on Ballerina.

"Charming couple." he said. "Though I do believe the girl will be obliged to eat her breakfast off the mantelpiece. Walloped the saddle at the trot."

"Poles all right?" Miss Wade asked, glancing at them.

"They'll do. I left the skewbald saddled for you."

"Right!" Miss Wade turned back to the stables and Tamzin said, "We don't know the first thing about bending."

"Joan and I'll give you a little demonstration then, shall we? Then you can have a slap at it yourselves. The main thing to remember is to keep your aids diagonal; left rein, right leg; right rein, left leg. Lean a little towards the pole you're rounding and mind your feet!"

The skewbald came dazzlingly across the field and followed the white mare through the poles. The two ponies stood watching with alert cocked ears, and intelligent faces poised. Tamzin and Rissa sat in their saddles, eagerly studying the technique of the matter. The horses circled at the end of the poles, threaded neatly through them again and turned towards the two ponies.

"Ready?" Mr. Randall said. "Rissa, you'd better take Cobweb first, and Tamzin, keep about three poles behind. Not too fast to begin with."

Rissa squeezed her calves and set off at a canter, Tamzin following some lengths behind. The dapple-grey pony got round three poles before Rissa realised that he was getting out of hand. She had been concentrating so hard on diagonal aids and not knocking the poles that she had forgotten his hatred of digging heels. His little ears were almost flat on his neck and his head thrown unnaturally high. Coming to the fourth pole he began to feel this was altogether too much and shot out at a tangent, shaking his head and galloping out across the paddock. Rissa suddenly realised what had been happening; remembered also what Miss Wade had said about pulling-up a runaway, and was thrilled to find that Cobweb responded almost at once to the pull-and-slacken of the reins.

She wheeled him back to the poles and saw Tamzin, still at a collected canter, turning for the homeward lap. She fell in behind, soberly determined to remember about the heels and to keep the little grey at a really slow canter this time. Consequently she got on much better and could hardly help a giggle of elation when Tamzin knocked the sixth pole over through rounding it too closely.

They pulled up beside the two horses and Miss Wade said, "I see you remembered what we were saying in the saddle-room, Rissa!"

"Yes! I *was* pleased with myself about it!" Rissa laughed.

Mr. Randall said it was a pretty good show, and

Tamzin still at a collected canter.

he'd noticed the lighter leg-work on the return journey. Not that this was needed or even advisable with most horses, he said, but Cobweb was funny about legs; and how about having another go at the poles? He swung himself from Ballerina's saddle, handed her reins to Miss Wade and went to replace the fallen pole.

This time they all went round the poles, in a drawn out string; first at a very slow canter and next time a little faster, till at the fourth time round they were moving pretty fast and throwing up mud. The two girls were beginning to laugh, as they were prone to at such moments, and eventually Tamzin's foot caught a pole and down it went again. They pulled up at the end of that lap and got their breath, the horses' ears flicking backwards and forwards in controlled excitement.

"Like to try the jumps?" Mr. Randall suggested.

The girls shot questioning glances towards the jumps. They were very low; barely a foot, they looked.

"We put them dead low for your first try," Miss Wade said, seeing the inquiring glances. "You mightn't even notice them if you're light on the ponies' mouths."

Mr. Randall nodded. "A jag on the reins upsets a pony's balance and makes him drop his hind legs. Think of the reins as if they were made of ribbon and likely to snap."

The girls nodded, their eyes on the jumps.

"And keep your weight forward. Don't let yourselves get left behind, so to speak. You'll be all right. Take it gently, no rushing. Joan and I'll give you a lead."

The four of them strung away to the first jump

at a slow canter. It was a low rail between a couple of posts, with two sheep-hurdles for wings. The big horses scarcely altered their stride for the lowly thing; Sea Pie cocked his ears and popped over without a check, but Tamzin lost a stirrup, found it again and cantered after the horses. Rissa, coming up behind, went over the rail all right, but a bit too fast and got slightly "left behind," jagging Cobweb's mouth a little in consequence. She collected herself on landing and followed Tamzin serenely over the second jump, a bundle of faggots set between hurdle-wings. The third jump was a natural ditch intersecting the field. Wings had been placed on the Hillocks side for them to jump through, but coming back they had to jump it again without the set-up hurdles. It was only about a yard across and the ponies took it in their stride, their riders hardly noticing any difference in movement as they went over.

The two horses appeared slightly shocked at the kind of jumps they had obviously been expected to take seriously, but the ponies had carried learners before and knew all about it.

"Round again?" Mr. Randall said, raising one eyebrow.

"Oh, YES!" Tamzin squeaked. She was reaping the advantages of learning on an almost perfect pony.

"Yes, please!" Rissa patted the grey pony's neck. "But may we go first this time, so that you can watch us and tell us how we managed? I'm sure I got what you called "left behind" when we jumped the rail."

"Certainly! But let Tamzin lead this time; her pony is quieter than yours. And you won't get left behind if you tip your weight far enough forward when your pony takes off, and don't let him rush."

They went round again, this time practically without incident, except that Tamzin misjudged the little ditch on the return jump and sat back with a wallop as the little bay flew over.

"We'll be able to pick out the little ditches on the inland rides for you now," Miss Wade told them as they trotted back to the stables.

"Don't forget Miss Polkinghorne at two," Mr. Randall said, leaning down to open the gate.

"Right! The Hay boy coming, too?"

"Yes, he'll have Sea Pie." he looked at his watch. "Time for a swim before lunch," he said. "Don't see why you shouldn't go with the girls, Joan. Won't take me long to do the horses."

Miss Wade dismounted and pushed back a lock of damp hair from her forehead. "Just what I could do with," she said. "It's sticky weather. Perhaps we can reverse the arrangement to-morrow and you go in?"

"Looks as if we might have all day to wallow in the waves, if you ask me. Rain blowing up, I should say."

He squinted at the sky, turned, and went in Ballerina's box.

"Dentist's this afternoon," Tamzin grumbled, carrying her tack into the saddle-room.

"You've nothing to complain of," Rissa said. "He only ever looks at them and says come again next holidays. Now if you had MY teeth . . ."

Tamzin ignored her. "And after that," she went on, wriggling into a smallish swim-suit, "we've got a person coming to tea. Someone Mummy used to know when they were at school. Must've been ages ago."

"Oh, come!" Miss Wade looked shocked. "You young people always seem to think folk are positively ancient at thirty or so!"

They walked barefooted over the dunes to the sea. The air was getting more and more oppressive, and not a sigh of wind to relieve the sticky heat. Even the sea was like warm liquid glass under the darkening sky.

"Storm coming," Rissa said, floating lazily.

"Shouldn't wonder," Joan Wade agreed. "And before evening."

It did come before evening, though it hung grumbling and scowling over a panting country till nearly tea-time. The immaculate Miss Polkinghorne got her pre-arranged ride, defying the thermometer in navy-blue serge and a bowler, though she did unbend towards her nephew's plight and let him leave his riding coat in the saddle-room.

Tamzin cycled the five miles to the dentist's and back without a drop from the brimming sky, but before she had been in the house ten minutes the whole village was blotted out by a wall of rain.

Mrs. Grey went upstairs and peered anxiously through the landing window into the veil of water. "Marjorie will be absolutely *soaked*," she kept saying to any one within earshot. "She was walking from the Saracen's Head."

Tamzin, staring into the grey blanket that was the Vicarage front garden, felt rather like a fish in an aquarium. One only had to pretend that the window wasn't there.

"Makes you think of the ancient days," Mr. Grey said, from the piano where he was going over hymns.

"Used to be sea right up to Dunsford once, and ships sailing over where this village is now. Battles fought right over our heads, so to speak."

Tamzin stared herself into a fantastic day-dream, where she was alternately a goggle-eyed fish and a mermaid, watching strange painted ships in ancient battles on the sea above Westling village.

Diccon got up from a train he was drawing on the *Church Times* under the laiden tea-table, and trotted to the piano where he liked to dive under a person's arm and play the middle bit. "Sing pussy song," he said, thumping middle C.

Mr. Grey obligingly ceased trying alternate tunes to "Now the Day is Over," and began on "Three Little Kittens" with Diccon still filling-in the middle bits according to his own ideas. It was at this point that Tamzin perceived a shape moving in the outer water. It glided to the porch and there, surprisingly, rang the bell. Tamzin and Mr. Grey went to the door, followed closely by Diccon and then Mrs. Grey. In the porch stood someone who looked as if she'd just risen, like Venus, from the foam, but complete with twentieth century dress and hat and handbag.

"Marjorie, my DEAR!" Mrs. Grey extended her hands, thought better of it and said, "Come along in and get some dry things on; I see we're still pretty much the same size. I can fit you out upstairs."

"I do feel ashamed of myself, arriving like this!" the shape beamed. "But I didn't expect THIS kind of welcome to Westling!"

She stepped out of a spreading pool of water into the hall, leaving a shining trail behind her like a human snail. Mrs. Grey relieved her of her outer belongings and Tamzin fetched her a pair of slippers.

Diccon dabbled his fingers in the shiny trail and
Mrs. Grey said, "Come along, my dear! Tamzin
will make tea, won't you, darling?" and led Venus
upstairs.

"Poor soul! Poor soul!" Mr. Grey muttered in his
kindly way, squeezing water out of a rose-pink
jacket into the kitchen sink.

Mrs. Grey led herself into the sitting-room for
tea—or so it seemed to Tamzin looking up at Venus
in Mrs. Grey's familiar blue linen frock and brown
sandals.

"Now I can introduce you properly! Richard,
Marjorie. Tamzin, come and meet Mrs. Tyrwhitt-
Price."

"Good-afternoon!" Tamzin said, and thought to
herself, "Did Mummy say Pricewhitt-Tyr? Or was
it Tyr-Price Whitt? I'll never remember a name like
that! Wish I could say Marjorie like she and Daddy
can."

They had a delightful meal with the delicious
Yorkshire tea-cakes Mrs. Grey was specially good
at, and the dark plum cake she made to her Scots
great-grandmother's recipe. And Mrs. Tyrwhitt-
Price revealed herself as a gorgeously jovial person
who told screamingly funny stories and thought
Diccon adorable.

Tamzin didn't join in the gusty conversation as
much as she would have liked because she was
terrified of mixing up the awful name. But when
her mother said towards the end of the meal, "Tamzin dear, pass the cake to Mrs. Tyrwhitt-Price,"
Venus laughed and said, "Don't saddle the child with
my deplorable married handle, Gwen! I've told
James more than once that I'd never have married
him if I hadn't been so frightfully fond of him.

Tamzin my dear, you call me Marjorie, like your mother!"

After tea they all helped to clear away the remnants and Marjorie shook the cloth in the hearth because, as she said, it would be pointless putting it out in all that rain, and did they mind if she smoked?

Neither of the Greys ever smoked, and this was Diccon's first really close view of the matter. He was enchanted from the first puff and came over to Marjorie's chair, his cornflower-blue eyes fixed unblinkingly on the tiny glowing circle. He leaned his arms on her knees and tilted his head, charmed with the whole procedure. Every time Marjorie removed the cigarette he solemnly intoned "More fire, Boy!" She blew smoke rings for him, and made a quite respectable impersonation of an engine going out of a station. She was bullied and coaxed into smoking three cigarettes in succession, and then declared herself beaten.

Mr. Grey gave a sudden guffaw, straightened his face as if he'd pulled a string to do it and said, "Gwenda my dear I can see we shall have to adopt the habit ourselves."

At bedtime that evening Tamzin blinked through the soap at her Mother, who was washing Diccon's socks in the bowl, and said, "WHAT did you say Marjorie's married name was?"

"Tyrwhitt-Price," Mrs. Grey replied, rubbing toes on heels.

"What did she used to be called?"

"Mingay. She was Marjorie Mingay at school."

Tamzin lay down in the steaming water and stared at her toes. "How dreadful for her!" she said. "Any one must love a man an awful lot to change

Mingay for Tyrwhitt-Price. It sounds so off-putting, as if she worked in a hospital or something forbidding like that. But Mingay sounds as if she were sitting all cosy by the fire, reading a book about horses."

Mrs. Grey squeezed out Diccon's socks, let the water go, and said, "You DO have funny ideas! Have you done your neck?"

CHAPTER EIGHT

AND THAT was the beginning of a week of gales such as hadn't been seen along that coast in any remembered August.

There was hardly any riding. Twice Tamzin took advantage of a dry interval to hurry across for a buffety ride in a wind like an express train, that blew sand over and into everything. Miss Wade remarked that even their eyelids seemed to grate when they blinked. It was a job to keep the horses exercised, and nearly all the bookings had to be cancelled.

Tamzin couldn't possibly have kept upright on her bicycle in the tearing wind, and had to walk along the sandy road with her head bent into the gale.

Rissa was pretty well stranded in Dunsford, there never being a long enough fine interval for her to walk the two-and-a-half miles to Westling and back again. There was only a bus on market-days and on this particular market-day it had been arranged that she must go with her mother to Hastings for the trying-on of winter school coats.

Tamzin read most of her favourite books again, and Mr. Grey suddenly decided to use the gale to advantage by re-distempering the attic bedroom. This opened up a new field of indoor activity for Tamzin who renovated the peeled-off paper horses, re-blacking them with Indian ink and tracing new horses to replace one or two torn ones that Diccon had got hold of.

"I should wait for dry weather before you try

sticking them up again," Mrs. Grey advised, so Tamzin spent another restless evening chafing at the unseasonable weather, the growing nearness of the gymkhana for which they couldn't practise, and the isolation of Rissa in the tidy Dunsford villa where she lived.

If anything the storm seemed worse. Staring listlessly out of the window, Tamzin saw a hen-house bowl along the shingle road in front of the Vicarage garden, a dustbin lid following shortly afterwards. The waves beyond the river mouth looked absolutely mountainous, even from the distance of the Vicarage. Tamzin left the dreary window-seat and went into the kitchen to find the black-board and chalks. They were spread all over the blue-and-white linoleum and Diccon was lying on his stomach in the midst, drawing wheels.

"Tamsie draw train, Boy!" he said with firm decision.

"Bother!" said Tamzin. "He would have the board! And he's got all day to use it if he wants."

"Well, so have you, at present," her mother pointed out from the table in the window where she was doing the family ironing.

"Oh well, I'll use a pencil. Could I have some paper?"

"Ask Daddy, dear. He might let you have some sermon-paper."

Tamzin trailed out of the kitchen and went in search of her father. She got the sermon-paper and drew Fallada all over it in every possible (and impossible) attitude till bedtime. And in bed that night the storm was so terrific that she could feel her lofty little room rocking shakily in the gale.

And somewhere in the blackest depths of the wild

Staring listlessly out of the window.

and dreadful night she heard a tremendous bang. She was out of bed almost as it happened for she knew what it was; she had heard it before. The lifeboat was going out, and they had just fired the maroon to call the crew.

Struggling into her dressing-gown, she fumbled her way to the window and looked out. She could see lanterns swinging round the Point, and as she stood there she saw the thin bright trail of a rocket, off Dunsmere Sands. People were moving below her in the house, and she stumbled downstairs towards the yellow light under her parents' door.

"Mummy, Daddy, may I come in?"

"Yes, come along," her father called back. He was

alone in the room, pulling a thick jersey over his shirt.

"Where's Mummy?"

"Gone to see if Diccon woke. Hadn't you better get back to bed? It's only half-past four."

"Oh, DADDY! Can't I come with you, PLEASE? I'll get dressed like lightning."

"But I'm going out to the lifeboat house. I couldn't possibly take you."

"Oh, DADDY!"

"And in this weather too! You'd be blown away. Mummy'll be glad of your help here; people may be brought in off the ship."

Mrs. Grey came in in her dark blue dressing-gown. "He hasn't stirred, so far as I can see," she said.

"Well I must hurry along. Tamzin will help you with blankets and things. Good-bye!" He was swallowed up in the shadows and Tamzin turned to her mother; "I did want to go too!" she said.

"I know, darling! But you wouldn't really want to if you knew that your being with Daddy might make him of less use to the others. Never mind! Come along in my bed for half an hour; there's time yet before we need get things ready."

Tamzin turned from the streaming window and padded across the room. "Yes, I see, Mummy. I didn't think of it just like that, but only how exciting it would have been. But you *are* right . . ." She climbed in bed beside her mother, feeling far too excited to sleep. She could hear the distant snarl of thunder above the uproarious racket of wind and rain, and rattling doors and windows.

"Just THINK of the lifeboat going out in this!" she said, wonderingly.

"And think of the ship," her mother said. "It's a

night for courage." She turned the little oil-lamp low in case of need and said, "Try to sleep for a little while."

But Tamzin couldn't. She was thinking of the ship, and what sort of people might be in her. Thinking of the lifeboat, and her father out on Dunsford Sands helping to launch her, in all the frenzy of the August gale.

At five o'clock Mrs. Grey turned up the lamp and Tamzin sat thankfully up. "I tried not to talk," she said. "But I just couldn't sleep a *wink*. Mummy, it must be two years since the lifeboat went out in weather like this; that time when the *Mazeppa* went down. It was in a November, wasn't it?"

"Yes, at the equinoctial tides. I don't think even this is as bad as the gale we had then."

Tamzin went up to find her clothes in the grey light of dawn. Nothing could be seen from her bedroom window; nothing but a driving veil of rain.

Downstairs she found her mother lighting the kitchen fire.

"You could hunt up the blankets, Tamzin," she said. "They're in the oak chest on the landing, and two more on the big spare bed."

Tamzin found them and spread them over a chair near the kitchen fire. Mrs. Grey was making cocoa in a large saucepan, and Tamzin put cups and saucers on the table and hunted round the house for more wooden chairs to add to the two in the kitchen.

At about a quarter to six the rain lifted, though the wind was as strong as ever. Tamzin ran up to her bedroom window and stared out over the river. She could see a small group of people against the lifeboat house; their coats were flapping in the wind and one

of them flung an arm out towards the sea. More
people surged out from inside the building and the
company moved down the shore. Straining her
eyes, Tamzin suddenly saw the gallant little lifeboat
lifted on the crest of a towering wave off-shore.

"Mummy! Mummy! They're coming in!" she
yelled.

Mrs. Grey ran upstairs. "Sh! You'll wake
Diccon!" she said, coming to the window.

"Oh, nothing wakes him, Mummy! But look,
they're coming in! Can you see the ship? Can you
see if there're people in the boat?"

Mrs. Grey peered through narrowed eyes. Tamzin
rubbed the window with her sleeve. "Shall I open
it?" she suggested.

"Great snakes! You'd be sucked up the chimney!"

"*Mummy!* You sound just like Rissa!"

"Well, I expect I'm catching the idiom from you
two slangy schoolgirls. There *are* people in the
boat, Tamzin, look! But I can't see any sign of a
ship."

The lifeboat came in closer to the shore, and the
watchers at the attic window saw a rope thrown,
caught and made fast. On the next wave the boat
appeared to be hurled among the people on the shore.
Ropes were tightened and men jumped over the
gunwale. Two heavy horses were led from the
shelter of the lifeboat house and hitched to the
ropes. They strained, and people gripped the ropes
and traces and strained too. The boat began to creep
up the shore, and when she was clear of the waves
the horses stopped pulling and a number of bundled
figures were helped and lifted down to waiting
groups on shore.

"Looks as if we'll need all our blankets," Mrs. Grey

said, watching the procession to the road where a lorry and a cart were waiting.

"Shall I take mine down too?" Tamzin offered.

"Yes, do. I'll go down and make up the fire. They'll be here in a few minutes."

Tamzin stripped her two blankets and caught up her mother in the hall. "Will they all be brought here?" she asked.

"I expect so. We're really the nearest big house and the nearest telephone. They're unlikely to attempt the distance to Dunsford with everyone soaked through, and it's a three-mile road on the other side of the river."

Mrs. Grey hung a pile of towels she had brought downstairs on the line above the fireplace, and went in search of jerseys and other spare garments. Diccon still slept on, and Tamzin hungrily devoured a plate of cornflakes, an apple and a glass of milk. She had barely swallowed the last gulp when her father opened the front door. She rushed into the hall and saw it filling with men of the lifeboat crew, most of them assisting or carrying a blanketed figure, and two of them manœuvring a stretcher to the stairs. Mrs. Grey came hurrying down with an armful of clothes and her husband smiled a little wearily and said, "I'm afraid this chap's pretty badly hurt. You've got the small spare bed made up?"

"Yes, it's all ready. You go up with them, Richard, and I'll manage in the kitchen."

Her father turned to the stretcher-bearers and said, "Second door on your right at the top of the stairs. I'll be up in a minute. Tamzin! Will you ring Dr. Hargreaves for me, please? Ask him to come here as soon as he can, and say it's a man brought in from a distressed vessel, and that we think he has a fractured hip. Dunsford 280. Good lass!"

Tamzin got her message through and went to the kitchen door. She knocked and called, "May I come in?"

Her mother came to the door and shut it behind her. "Would you go first to the Institute and ask Mrs. Clench if she can give you the trousers and guernseys from the emergency box over the billiard room? And if there are socks we must have them too. There *should* be six pairs."

"Yes, Mummy. Trousers, guernseys and socks." Tamzin got into her coat, tied a scarf over her head because of the wind, and went out. The sky was clearing, and the wind perhaps a shade less violent though it was still strong enough to beat Tamzin sideways into the tamarisks before she had time to adjust her balance. She was blown to the Institute like a November leaf and knocked on the caretaker's door. Mrs. Clench opened it a crack because of the gale, recognised Tamzin and said, "Come IN, dearie! You'll be wantin' they trowsis? Ee! but it's good to know they're all safe 'ome, the lads."

In Mrs. Clench's kitchen Tamzin knelt to play with an albino cat which had pink eyes and nose and paws. It was said to be twenty years old and to have come off a shipwrecked schooner when Mrs. Clench was young.

"Now, duckie, here you are! Three pair er trowsis (one bein' too bad with the moth) four guernseys, six pair er socks and I've put in some thick pants of Albert's; I reckon yer ma'll be glad of them an' I'll get 'em back before the frost."

She piled the things on the table beside a heap of windfall apples and a rolling-pin.

"Thank you very much, Mrs. Clench, and how is Mr. Clench?" Tamzin gathered up the pile.

"Middlin', Missy, middlin'. 'Is trouble is Westling do fly to 'is chest so. It's on account of its bein' so wet and low, see, but a break in the weather'll set 'im up proper."

Tamzin said good-bye and struggled home against the whipping wind with her load before her. She went in the back door, through the scullery and knocked. Her mother opened the kitchen door and said, "Come in and meet our guests!" She took the trousers and guernseys and placed them over the rail of the fireguard, while Tamzin stood hesitating shyly before the blanketed seamen gathered round the kitchen stove with steaming cups of cocoa in their hands. All were strangers, since the lifeboat crew had gone to their own cottages where dry clothes and hot breakfasts were awaiting them.

The men turned and smiled at her through varying growths of beard. She smiled back and heard her mother say, "This is my daughter Tamzin. And, Tamzin, this is the skipper and crew of the cargo boat *Capella*. Come and have some cocoa with us."

Tamzin came and sat on the edge of the table between a jar of Demerara sugar and the breadboard. The skipper, swathed in a pink blanket, glanced up at her with a friendly grin. He had a shock of wild black hair, a leathery skin and penetrating blue eyes. He balanced his cocoa in his left hand because his right was completely hidden in a padded bandage.

"Are you very much hurt?" Tamzin asked, with sudden concern.

"Not much more'n a scratch. But it's a little stiff you know." The skipper's voice was resonant and seemed to fill the kitchen up, though Tamzin had the impression that he was talking quietly, for him.

"And the man upstairs? Will he be all right do you think?"

"Well, Missy, he likely will. Can't say very much till doctor comes. Poor feller went overboard and were dashed against the boat. Hip, we reckon. Nice chap; wireless operator."

"Isn't that a car, now?" Mrs. Grey said, pausing in her ladling of hot porridge. The door-bell rang, and Tamzin said, "I'll take him up," and slithered from the table.

She was back in a couple of minutes. "It was him," she said. "And he wants to look at everyone before he goes."

"Well, let's have something hot to eat in the interval," Mrs. Grey said, spooning brown sugar on to plates of oatmeal porridge. Tamzin poured hot milk over and carried plates round.

"Diccon was awake. I heard him talking to his Teddy when I was coming downstairs," she added.

"Then I'll have to leave you all to manage by yourselves, and get him up," Mrs. Grey said, picking up Diccon's orange juice and departing by the hall door.

Tamzin ladled a small plate of porridge for herself and sat down with it beside a seaman with curly red hair and her own green blanket round his knees. "I had cornflakes before you came," she said. "But I still feel hungry. I seem to have been up ages."

"I bin up all night," he told her, blowing gently on his porridge, "'Fact we all have."

"You must be awfully tired! I saw you all coming

in, from my attic window. But I couldn't see your ship anywhere."

"She went down. Five minutes after the last of us left her."

Tamzin put her loaded spoonful back in her plate. "Oh, dear! I'm so SORRY!" she said, as if the ship had been the red-haired seaman's wife or mother.

He shrugged his eyebrows. "'S life, Missy. She were the second wreck I bin in, both lost. Plenty more ships still."

"Yes, I suppose so," Tamzin seemed uncertain. "What did you used to do in the ship? She was a tramp, wasn't she?"

A wiry little sailor next to the skipper leaned forward and pointed his spoon. "I'll tell you wot 'e did aboard the blinkin' *Capella*. Made experiments on us, 'e did, in fancy cookin'. Wants to be a proper smart chef chap in one er they posh liners, does Bert. Not in my line, this la-de-da cookery-wookery."

Bert laughed good-naturedly and told Tamzin to take no notice of Tom, he was so ignorant he couldn't even cook water.

"Well, I don't much like cooking, myself," Tamzin admitted. "Except fudge and pancakes, and perhaps fritters because it's nice fishing them out. But what I really want to know is what kinds of things you had in the ship; what sort of cargo I mean. Did you carry lots of exciting things like in Masefield's song; you know, peacocks and apes and ivory, and things like that? Or just something dull like fertiliser and timber?"

Bert gave a loud guffaw. "Apes," he said, "Peacocks! Not on yer life, Missy. Not on no ship where I'm in. We carried coffee and pepper. From Java and Borneo, we gottem."

"And'll litter up your nice sands somethin' shockin', I'll bet," Tom remarked.

They all looked up at a knock on the kitchen door and saw Dr. Hargreaves walking in. He smiled at Tamzin and said she was wanted in the dining-room.

"I'll come back later on," she said to Bert, and shut the door behind her. Mr. Grey was busy at the telephone as she went through the hall and into the dining-room where Mrs. Grey was tying on Diccon's bib for his breakfast.

"Could you help him with this, darling?" she said. "Dr. Hargreaves will have to make an emergency operation upstairs, and I shall have to help."

"Yes, of course, Mummy darling! Tamsie butter Boy's toast?" she offered, sitting down by Diccon.

"Boy no toast. Boy salt!" Diccon said firmly.

"Well, perhaps just a *little*," Tamzin said, dropping a couple of grains on the toast with a great deal of flourish.

CHAPTER NINE

BY THE next morning the gale had blown itself out.
There was hardly a stir in the trees outside Tamzin's
lofty window. The sky was clear and the day looked
promising. She dressed cheerfully, with her window
flung wide open for the first time for almost a week.
Glancing critically at her newly distempered walls
she decided they ought to be perfectly all right for
her to stick up the black horses in the evening. She
left her door propped open to allow a current of
warm air to flow through from the big south window
and hurried quietly downstairs. Past the small spare
room she went on tip-toe, hardly breathing, because
the wireless operator from *Capella* was still there
with a compound fracture of the hip, and could not
possibly be moved. All the other men had departed
on an evening train from Dunsford, except for one
who was taken to Dunsford Cottage Hospital with
an injury to his foot. They had spent most of the
previous day sleeping on camp beds at the Sailors'
Institute, and Tamzin had helped at the grand
farewell tea the village people spread for them on
the billiard table.

The Vicarage seemed oddly quiet this morning
after the stir and talk and laughter of yesterday's
crowded breakfast hour. Even Diccon was being
kept from the bedrooms and hall, and had been
encouraged to make a mess with chalks instead of
walking around dragging the tin tray behind him,
which had been his first idea.

Tamzin helped to prepare a breakfast tray for the
unseen guest, whose name was Laurence Hunter.

She would have liked to take it up but Mrs. Grey said better not, just yet; he wasn't up to seeing any more strange faces. Perhaps in a day or two. Tamzin tried to imagine what kind of a man he might be. "What does he *look* like?" she asked.

"Oh, youngish. Quite an ordinary kind of face, but nice. Brown eyes and hair."

"Could I pick some flowers for him? Just some tiny ones for his tray?"

"Yes, I should think he might like that. But you'll have to be quick; I want to take it up in a minute."

Tamzin picked a handful of white allysum and sky-blue flax. They did look perfect together, and she put them in a little brown cream jug on the breakfast tray.

"I'll take them up with your good wishes, shall I?" Mrs. Grey suggested, picking up the tray.

"Oh yes! And say I shall bring some myself when he's well enough for visitors."

Rissa arrived before breakfast was properly over, and bombarded Tamzin with questions. She helped with the clearing and washing up, which Tamzin had offered to do because her mother was having to include the duties of nurse in her already full day, and listened enthralled to Tamzin's account of the Friday's adventures.

"The skipper sounds nice," she said. "But if I'd been you I'd have asked him to *show* me the tattooed ship on his chest."

"It wouldn't have been very polite."

"Sailors aren't polite; they scorn that kind of thing. Look how you said they blew on their porridge. That isn't polite."

"Well, never mind. I was going to tell you about his hand."

"Oh yes! The one in the padded bandage. Was it really only a scratch?"

"Mummy told me the doctor said it was crushed. Quite badly, the whole hand. He said the skipper must have been in frightful pain, but he didn't even seem to notice it when I was there."

"How awful!" Rissa said. "What happened?"

"He got it trapped between the lifeboat and the tramp. There was a terrific sea you know, and the boats were just thrown about."

"You do have exciting things happen to you, Tam! Fancy me missing all this! I'd have come down before but Mummy said I'd get wet and everything—you know how it is." She sighed. "It isn't as if I hadn't got waterproofs."

"I was sorry you missed it, too."

"Oh, but I nearly forgot to tell you! There's one thing I *haven't* missed; I'm going to have jodhpurs!"

"Rissa!"

"Yes, really. When I told Daddy about the gymkhana and everything, he said, ' you can't possibly go in shorts and things; you'll have to have breeches,' before I even mentioned them. So I said certainly every one else would have riding clothes and if I could, too, may I have jodhpurs because you don't need riding boots for them. And he said he'd never heard of them, but if they were the correct thing they were all right. Mummy said she thought it was a needless expense, just for a gymkhana, but Daddy said if his daughter was going to ride a decent pony at Dunsford Gymkhana she was doing it properly, and he wasn't going to feel ashamed before all his friends. Marvellous, isn't it? I never thought I'd get them."

"Quite marvellous, and I'm almost certain I'll

never get mine. I haven't dared even to mention them, yet; so many bills seem to come in almost every post, unless they're receipts which doesn't really seem likely. And no one's ever asked what I'M going to wear at the gymkhana."

Rissa laid down the last fork, hung up the tea towel and said, "Don't get so downhearted. Something will turn up."

"There isn't such an awful long time for it to turn in," Tamzin sighed. She dried her hands on the roller towel and followed Rissa into the garden. "Did you remember to wish at the gate?" she asked, pumping her front tyre which had a slow puncture.

"Yes, of course! But you know, I sometimes think it's pretty childish."

"Well, we're children, aren't we?"

"Perhaps you feel that way at ten, but when you've got to eleven——"

"Rissa! You pig!"

They pedalled down to the ferry and whistled for Old Jim. He was having his breakfast in his hut, and came out wiping his beard on a large spotted handkerchief.

"Mornin', strangers," he said, handing bicycles into his boat as if they had been handbags.

"Well, I've been over twice this week, Jim. I can't be very strange," Tamzin said, bracing herself against the bicycles.

"Oh, ah! 'Cleanin' tack,' you said you was? Reckon you're off a bit earlier when it looks like there bein' a bit more ridin'."

Tamzin felt this was uncalled-for, and said nothing. In any case, how could one explain parents' decisions to Jim? It was impossible even to imagine him ever having *had* a parent.

"How's the patient?" Jim offered, trying again.

"Pretty bad at the moment, but Daddy says Dr. Hargreaves thinks he'll be all right. He may be at our house for weeks, but so far I haven't even seen him—except going upstairs on a stretcher."

"Reckon they want to spare 'im shock, pore feller," Jim remarked, and Tamzin decided he was feeling crusty this morning and ought to be checked. "Is your rheumatism bad this morning, Jim?" she said sweetly. "I expect it IS a bit tiresome after rough weather!"

Jim shot one eyebrow up to his scalp and busied himself with backing his little boat to the Dunsmere steps.

"Careful with them bikes!" he said, as the girls hoisted them off the thwarts. "Let me 'eave 'em up, or I'll be 'aving you drowned on me 'ands. Not so young as I was fer swimmin'. Time was when it were different, though, Ah!"

Tamzin bristled. "We're perfectly at home in the water, and you know it, Jim!" she retorted.

"Did you used to swim a lot, Jim?" Rissa asked, steering the conversation to smoother channels and holding the stern of the boat steady with her toe.

"Swim? Aye! Dive and all. Use ter go off cross-tree of me Dad's smack. Saw a man try it one time; 'e weren't so lucky. Split himself from top to bottom, ah!"

"How dreadful, Jim! Was he killed?"

"Oh, ah!" Jim pocketed their pennies and swung himself down into his boat with astonishing ease for so very old a man. He bent to his oars, his white hair silver in the morning sun, and his little brass ear-rings winking and flashing as he swayed.

Tamzin wondered if he took them off to polish them, as she pedalled after Rissa down the sandy road.

John Starling was sitting on his gate, and accosted them as they laboured past in the wind-blown sand that had banked on the Dunsmere roads. "Aren't you coming in to leave your bicycles?" he called, in surprised disappointment.

"Not to-day, John. We're leaving them at the stables."

"Oh, and I wanted to show you Mina's young!" his voice wailed after them. "Will you come in on your way home?"

"All right!" Rissa shouted over her shoulder, turning up the Hillocks track.

"Rissa! Now you've done it!" Tamzin said despairingly.

"Oh, never mind! It keeps him happy and won't take us a minute."

"The dear little bunnies!" Tamzin said, with some sarcasm.

They found Miss Wade still 'mucking out' the stables. "I'm late this morning," she said. "I would be, just when we've got to get to the forge."

"Do let us help with that!" Rissa said.

"Would you like to wheel this lot round to the muck heap, then?"

Rissa seized the barrow handles and trundled purposefully away. Tamzin was given a large old sponge to clean out the mangers, and then they all carried water from Mr. Murphy's.

"Mr. Randall is out with the holiday couple who came the day the storm began," Miss Wade said. "But when he gets back we have to take Allegro and Timpani to the forge at Dunsford. Would you like to ride Timpani, Rissa? Tamzin could come along

" I wanted to show you Mina's young."

on the bay pony; he doesn't need shoeing but he can do with the exercise after a week mostly in stables."

The girls were delighted at the prospect of riding again and got busy grooming the ponies; Miss Wade said they hadn't been properly strapped, she having been delayed over a hitch with the chaff-cutting machine.

Tamzin shouted details of the lifeboat affair into the next box where Miss Wade was forking bedding, and Rissa bawled the news about her jodhpurs in the intervals when Tamzin was getting breath.

They were ready and waiting when the three horses appeared at the gate. The holiday couple were looking very pleased with themselves and said, How about Monday morning at the same time? This was agreed upon and they patted their horses' necks while Joan Wade altered Timpani's leathers, and the young woman confided with suppressed pride that she had just learned to rise at the trot.

The ride to Dunsford was delightful; the air heady after the clean sweep of the storm, and the brown August turf already showing a brighter green. They cantered and trotted gaily along the short-cut through the fields, across wooden foot-bridges spanning marsh ditches, and over saltings quite blue with sea holly and viper's bugloss. The horses were interested in the ride and keen to go, after their inactive days. None of them had loose shoes, and were only making a routine visit to the forge for foot trimming and overhaul, so were allowed to canter freely on the springy turf.

Dunsford's ancient houses glowed rose-red in the warm sunshine, and the blue-cobbled streets echoed cheerily to the horses' feet. At the forge the three horses were hitched to iron rings, one inside and two under trees beside the door. Joan Wade stayed with Allegro in the smithy, and the two girls leaned over the iron railings that ran along the edge of the inland cliff on which the town was built. They could see for miles across the marshes, beyond Westling and Dunsmere to the sea horizon.

"Just perfect to-day, isn't it?" Tamzin sighed

happily, leaning her chin on her arms and gazing lovingly at the spread out marshes dotted with tree-girdled farmsteads and flocks of grazing sheep; at the huddled villages and shining, rolling sea.

"Bit of a swell on, still," Rissa observed practically.

"Makes you want to write poetry," Tamzin said, clinging to her happy mood.

"Well, WELL now! If it isn't dear little Tamzin!" a loud and hearty voice accosted her unwilling ear. "Oh, and Rissa too! JUST the people I've been wanting! I'm sure you're JUST the two to help me in my little dilemma, ha-ha!"

They turned to see the overflowing figure of Mrs. Egbert Hickey, a celebrated member of practically every local committee and absolutely bursting with good works. Though not in Westling parish, being a Dunsford resident, she had a finger in every surrounding pie, and was in her element giving little addresses to Mrs. Grey's "mothers" or encouraging the Dunsmere women to contrive respectable seersucker dresses for half-clad Pacific island natives. The trouble was she had no children of her own and was too well-off to have any domestic occupations in her own immaculate house.

"Now what would you say to a jolly afternoon in Hastings? No, no!" she raised a large gloved hand as Rissa began to say, "Well, we were really going to practise for the gymkh——"

"No polite refusals needed with ME, my dears! You know I don't stand on ceremony. You shall have ices at Pepini's and éclairs at the Devonshire. And you can go to the Silver Greyhound bus *directly* you've had your dinners."

"It's very kind of you, Mrs. Hickey, but the fact is——" Tamzin began.

"Oh, you don't have to thank ME, my dear," Mrs. Hickey boomed, giving Tamzin a playful prod with the parrot's head handle of her umbrella. "You'll be doing me a little kindness in return, you know! I want you to leave a little parcel for me at Lady Whapshott's jumble sale in St. Chad's Church Room. I promised dear Agnes a few things for the sale some *weeks* ago, and—well, you know what a busy woman I am!" she smiled roguishly. "What with one thing and another I forgot all *about* them, till dear Agnes rang up at breakfast and said the sale was this *afternoon.* Of course I can't possibly take them myself; I'm speaking a few words to the Guild of Nimble Knitters at three prompt. And naturally I couldn't dream of letting dear Lady Whapshott down, especially as the sale is for one of my most *deserving* good causes; the Society for Supplying Servicable Shirts to Samoans. A *very* needy work! Well, it is so good of you two kiddies to help me out like this! It is *such* a relief, you know! I'll have the little parcel ready by two o'clock, and I won't forget the éclairs and ices. GOOD-bye, my dears! Give my *dearest* love to your dear mother, Tamzin. It is SO nice of you both——" She turned down the hill like a steam-roller in party dress and vanished in a flurry of mauve muslin round the corner.

"WELL!" said Rissa, recovering.

"Phew!" said Tamzin. "Bang goes our lovely afternoon."

"Eclairs and ices!" Rissa said with deep disgust.

"Well *they're* all right, aren't they?"

"It's like selling your soul for the sake of your stomach."

"Well, not our souls, quite," Tamzin quibbled.

"Split-hairer!" Rissa accused, turning to see how the shoeing was going on.

Accordingly, they were sitting in the two-fifteen Silver Greyhound that afternoon with disconsolate faces, an enormous parcel of Mrs. Egbert Hickey's fantastic cast-off clothing and a mauve envelope which was flourishingly inscribed "Tickets and a Good Time for the Kiddies."

"Horrible word, 'kiddies!'" Rissa grumbled, staring aggressively at the envelope.

"M'm. Like calling bitches 'lady-dogs,'" Tamzin agreed.

"Have you thought what a gorgeous time we could have dressing up in all these preposterous things?" Rissa suddenly said.

"How do you know they're preposterous?"

"Sure to be. All her things always are. Look at that puce gown with black snakes all over it that she wore for mother's Garden Party. Bet it's in here."

Tamzin giggled. "How do you suppose she'd dress her children if she had any?"

Rissa's eyebrows shot up. "Doesn't bear thinking of," she said. "Mercy she hasn't. Though I dare say she really means well."

They arrived in Hastings well before three and staggered hilariously through the disinterested August crowds supporting the unspeakable parcel between them. Mrs. Hickey's packing was not what one would call efficient, and the eccentric contents were soon bursting from their wrappings in every direction.

Something long and flamboyantly orange was pouring over Tamzin's shoulder, and Rissa was frantically collecting endless streamers of green-and-red striped satin from a widening slit in her side of the parcel.

At St. Chad's Church Room they had to support themselves against the outer wall for a minute to collect their mirth-scattered wits and wipe the tears of helpless laughter from their faces. They pulled their mouths into sedate lines, stuffed the frothing garments back into their holes as best they could, and marched into the Church Room behind a towering mountain of a woman with five children in tow.

"Ask *her*!" Tamzin whispered, nodding towards a tired-looking elderly woman behind the footwear stall.

They asked, and the tired woman said, "Lady Whapshott? Why yes, she was here a moment ago. I don't expect she'll be long. Her stall is over in that corner under the window; would you like to wait there a moment?"

They heaved the abandoned collection of paper, garments and string across to the corner stall, and leaned against the trestle table watching the milling crowd of Old Town mothers inspecting the goods set out around the room. Tamzin, turning to whisper to Rissa, saw something faintly familiar out of the corner of her eye. She screwed round and looked at the object squarely. It was a pointed shape of buckskin, protruding from a foam of dresses and petticoats and jerseys on Lady Whapshott's stall. Tamzin stared at it for a moment, vaguely wondering what it was reminding her off; suddenly recalled Miss Wade in riding togs and knew. She dived on to the buckskin like a terrier on a rat, and tore out a pair of brown whipcord jodhpurs.

" They're just my size and everything."

"Rissa, LOOK!" she shrieked, brandishing the garment like a war flag.

A hush fell on the room and people turned and stared curiously at the stall. There were others turning the Whapshott articles over for inspection, and Tamzin tried to look as if it had not been *her* who had shrieked. Then she suddenly realised that Rissa was handing over the disreputable parcel to a person who had appeared behind the counter and was saying, "Oh, Arabella's parcel, is it not?"

Tamzin clung to the jodhpurs saying over and over in her mind, "I *must* get them, I must, I must, I MUST! They're just my size and everything; I must, I must, I MUST!" She held them out and said firmly and clearly, "How much are these, please?"

Dear Agnes looked slightly shocked and said, "Aren't you the little girl from Westling Vicarage? They're—let me see—four-and-six."

Tamzin's mind worked more rapidly than it had ever done in her life before. She looked up and said, "Is there a telephone near here?"

"Why, yes; there's a box just down the road," Lady Whapshott replied, looking curiously at her.

"Well would you mind if I just went and rang up Mummy to ask if I can have them? I won't be long —only you see we haven't enough money with us now; only a shilling each for ices and buns."

"Well, yes, I should think you could do that. Did you know there was a jacket to go with them? No? I saw it somewhere——" She rummaged obligingly and produced a neat little tailored riding coat in ginger Harris tweed. She peered at the ticket and pronounced that the price was marked five shillings.

"I expect I shall wake up in a minute," Tamzin

said. "It's a most *heavenly* little jacket! Could you change my shilling into pennies for the phone, do you think?"

Lady Whapshott changed it and Tamzin tore through the crowd of hopeful mothers and out of the double door. She got her number and posted pennies in the slot. "Is that you, Mummy? This is Tamzin. There's a pair of marvellous jodhs and a jacket at this sale, just my size. PLEASE could I have them? They're four-and-six and five shillings, and I'll let them be my birthday and Christmas presents, only PLEASE let me have them!"

"But darling, I couldn't *think* of it! They might have come from anywhere. You could get all sorts of things from them. I'm sorry, darling, *very* sorry, but I couldn't hear of it."

Tamzin trailed dejectedly back to the sale. The bottom of her world had gone in splinters. High hopes had crashed from the stars and crept below earth. She dragged her feet sadly back to the stall and said in a small voice, "I can't. She says they might have come from anywhere and I could get anything from them."

Dear Agnes handed a flannel petticoat and sixpence change to a granny in a black bonnet, and turned to Tamzin. "They mightn't, and you won't!" she hissed in Tamzin's ear. "I know where they came from. You run along and tell your mother they belonged to the youngest daughter of the Countess Alexandrina de Sacré, and I'll guarantee them as absolutely *immaculate*. You'll want some more pennies; here you are. Now run along!"

Tamzin's face lit up with a sudden surge of wild hope. She said, "Oh, THANK you!" and turned and ran.

Mrs. Grey listened in doubtful silence to this new appeal and said a little less firmly, "Well, I still say that you can never be sure, even from a Countess. However . . ."

"Yes, Mummy?"

"However, perhaps we'll say yes this time, on condition that they go *straight* to the cleaners."

"Oh Mummy, you angel darling *sweetest* Mummy, I'll love you for ever!" Tamzin banged down the receiver and charged joyously back to Dear Agnes.

"I can, I can, I CAN!" she said, and then saw the boy in the raincoat. He had the jodhpurs in his hands —HER jodhpurs. And Rissa hadn't even noticed; she was helping Lady Whapshott do up parcels.

"Those are MINE!" Tamzin said sharply, with a sudden pang.

"Oh, yeah? It don't say ' sold ' on 'em nowheres, and they lay 'ere among the rest. So what?" He turned to Rissa behind the counter. "I'll 'ave 'em, Miss. They'll do nice fer gardenin'."

"Don't Rissa! Tell him they're mine!" Tamzin was anguished.

"You paid for them?" the boy asked truculently. "My money's on the counter, see?"

Tamzin opened her mouth, stared at the coins, shut it and looked despairingly at Dear Agnes. And she, valiant soul, suddenly realised what was going on and swept purposefully down to their end of the stall. "Paid for?" she said to the aggressive youth. "Did you say were they *paid* for? Indeed they are! I've paid for them myself, five minutes ago; I want them for a present. You were just too late; I'm so sorry!"

The boy in the raincoat glowered, tossed down the jodhpurs and stalked away without a word.

"Now, my dear," Lady Whapshott turned to Tamzin, "allow me to make you a little present in return for coming all this way in time for my sale. Since your mother approves, I feel quite free to hand them to you with my thanks. And Rissa, my dear, there'll be a little thing for you in the post. I'll send it to Tamzin for you. Don't bother to thank me, now! Off you go and get your ice-creams!"

They went. "Come on now!" Tamzin exulted. "Let's go and have a smashing blow-out!"

CHAPTER TEN

THE WEEK after the jumble sale was just as perfect and summery as the previous one had been wild and wintery. Tamzin was so happy she almost ached with it. She and Rissa practically lived at the stables, except for one afternoon taking Dunsford Dairy ponies to the forge because, as Rissa pointed out, they mustn't burn their boats for the winter when Hillocks would be back in Tonbridge. And even Dairy ponies were *ponies* and much better than no riding at all.

At Hillocks Stables they did everything from cleaning tack and mucking out stables to gymkhana practice and riding with the others whenever there were mounts to spare. They even swam the horses twice, on glorious early mornings when the sands were almost empty of people, and the ponies could gallop freely from the sea without danger to toddlers and family parties.

The bending practice was becoming a fast and exciting affair at which the girls were beginning to show some skill. Even the jumps had gone up by nearly as much again, and they had erected a low cardboard wall in front of the " water jump."

The gymkhana schedules had arrived, and were already much-thumbed and studied by every one at Hillocks. The two girls were entered for four classes; " Child's best pony, not exceeding thirteen-two hands," " Musical Chairs," " Walk, Trot, Mount and Gallop," and " Bending," the three last-named events for children under twelve. For " Child's best pony" they had been practising cantering in a figure of eight and were getting tolerably efficient, though found it difficult to get their ponies to change legs in the middle; especially Rissa who was handicapped by Cobweb's ticklish horror of heels.

Joan Wade and Mr. Randall were both in the Open Jumping on Timpani and Ballerina, and Mr. Randall was riding Allegro in the Handy Hunter class and Ballerina in the Wheelbarrow Race.

There had been a great deal of anxiety over jodhpurs; would they be ready in time for the Day? Rissa's were still in the back-room of the local tailor who was making them, and all Tamzin had to show was a ticket from the cleaners. On the Saturday morning, however, Rissa arrived with a parcel tied to her carrier. Tamzin rushed out to meet her and shouted, "You've got your jodhs!"

"No, yours!"

"What do you mean, mine?"

"I went in to the cleaners just to see if yours *were* done, and they were. So I brought them. I had mine fitted when I got home yesterday, and he says I can have them to-night, whoopee!"

Tamzin fell on the parcel and bolted up to her room, with Rissa on her heels and Diccon stumping breathlessly in the rear. Her clothes fairly shot to the floor, and she bumped down on top of them to get into her jodhpurs. Diccon came puffing into the room and said, "Got twowsis on!" to Tamzin in a surprised tone of voice. He climbed on her bed and sat watching with absorbed interest.

"All I want now is a hat," Tamzin said, buttoning the ginger Harris jacket. "Do they look nice, Riss?"

"Smashing!" Rissa said characteristically. It was her strongest word.

"Let's go down and look in Mummy's long mirror; come on, Diccon!"

She helped him down and burst into her mother's room. Mrs. Grey was making the bed. "Tamzin, my dear, how delightful!" she exclaimed, straightening up and appraising the outfit. "It really might have been made for you. A little brown felt hat would make it perfect!"

"I just said that to Rissa!"

"Well, I'll see if I can find one that would do for riding and for church in the winter, too. You do need a new one for church, anyhow."

Tamzin bounced over the bed and hugged her mother boisterously round the waist. "And may we use your mirror?" she asked, using it. "Golly! It DOES look marvellous, doesn't it? I can use my crop now, too!"

Mrs. Grey plumped up pillows and said, "Have you given Rissa her parcel?"

"Heavens, no! I forgot!"

"You know Daddy doesn't like you saying 'Heavens,' Tamzin."

"Heavens! So he doesn't! I mean, Crikey, so he doesn't. Sorry, Mummy! Come on, Rissa!"

They surged to the door and Mrs. Grey called after them, "Not too much noise past Laurie's door!"

"All right, Mummy; may I show him too?"

"Yes, do! But don't forget to knock!"

"My parcel first!" Rissa stated flatly.

"Oh all right then; come on!" Down they went with jumps and bounds, Diccon following doggedly, coming stern first on all fours.

"Here it is!"

Rissa pushed the string over the corner of the

little parcel and jerked it off. "I'll bet it's from Dear Agnes," she said, tearing at the paper.

"Don't you dare to make fun of her!" Tamzin warned. "If it hadn't been for her I'd have been stranded in my shorts for Wednesday."

Rissa pulled out a little wooden box with the lid tacked down. Tamzin ran into the kitchen for a screwdriver and they levered it up. From a deep bed of shavings and cotton wool Rissa withdrew a little plaster figure of a horse. It was quite exquisite, in conformation and poise. The horse's head was alertly turned to see something happening behind him; his spine curved delicately to the sweep of his neck and his tail held like a banner to balance the curve. In every detail the figure was perfection. Rissa set it on the hall dresser shelf, and the girls stood and stared in profound appreciation.

"He's just perfect. He's like a horse in a legend," Rissa said.

"And he's a beginning for your horsy bedroom. A simply gorgeous one, too."

Diccon reached up for the wooden box and it fell with a thud on the floor, spilling shavings and cotton wool.

"Look, there's a note," Tamzin said, and picked it up. Rissa read it and said, "It IS Lady Whapshott. She sends her love to you and Diccon."

Tamzin picked the little boy up and said, "Lady Whapshott sends you her love, Diccon!"

"Washpot send Diccon gloves. You give me!"

Tamzin giggled. "Isn't he gorgeous? Come on and see Laurie. Did I tell you his parents came to see him on Wednesday?"

"What, all the way from Yorkshire?"

"Of course. They'd have come from Scotland if

they'd lived there. They think the world of him."

"Well, he IS nice," Rissa said.

"I know he is. Let's leave Diccon with Mummy; he's not really supposed to go in Laurie's room without her in case he bumps into his plaster or anything."

Mrs. Grey took her son downstairs and Tamzin knocked on Laurence Hunter's door. "It's Tamzin and Rissa!" she called. "NOT the doctor or anything like that."

"Come in!"

They did. Laurence was lying flat, half-encased in his plaster; his bed beside the south-east window where he could watch the fishing boats sail in and out of Westling Harbour, and the coming and going of fishermen round the Point. He had grown a fine brown beard and smiled at the girls from its depths.

"Tamzin, you look smashing!" he said. "If I've got the right word?"

"Laurie, stop teasing and say if you really like it."

"Of course I do. I just said so."

"You were laughing at me. I never know when to take you seriously."

"All right my child. I think you look charming! That do? I really did mean it."

"Thank you, Laurie, but I'm *not* your child all the same."

Laurence twinkled at Rissa. "She does bully me, you know!" he said. "Tam, come and sit down here beside me. Was there anything in the post for me this morning?"

"Of course not, Laurie. I'd have brought it if there were." She sat astride the chair and took an apple from his bowl.

"You forgot once," he reminded.

"Shall I peel you an apple?" she suggested, skirting his remark.

"You can pass me one, but you ought to know by now that I like 'em with their peel *on*."

Rissa held out her little plaster horse and said, "Isn't he perfectly lovely?"

Laurence screwed round his head. "Put him on the window seat where I can see him properly," he said.

Rissa stood him on the seat and sat down beside him. Laurence studied the figure critically for a moment and said, "He certainly *is* perfectly lovely, as you say. In fact, I should imagine you've got something pretty valuable there. The modelling is beautifully done, and the whole thing is so balanced."

"He came from Lady Whapshott—you remember? At the jumble sale."

"And Laurie!" Tamzin interrupted, "Diccon called her ' Washpot! ' Isn't he wonderful? I'd never have thought of it."

"Diccon's a stout chap," Laurence said, "though disrespectful."

Rissa was staring out across the Harbour. "I don't think I'd really like to go to sea," she said. "Think of no horses for weeks on end!"

"The sea is to some people what horses are to you, though," Laurence said. "And one feels ' Fancy no sea for weeks on end! ' It's rather like a magnet, and one always goes back to it, even though one knows just how dangerous and uncomfortable and how lonely and monotonous it can be."

"Yes, I think I see," Rissa said. "But I'm so much on the side of the horses that I still find it difficult to understand your point of view."

Tamzin finished her apple and threw the core out

E

of the open window. "Ought to be going," she said, standing up. "Anything we can bring you first, Laurie?"

"I don't think so, thanks, except to pass me my pencil and pad. I could have another go at sketching, but it does come wonky, on my back."

"Sketch some horses!" Rissa said.

"He never does anything but ships," Tamzin complained, passing the pad.

"That, Miss Grey, is a lie," Laurence remarked.

"Well, practically never," Tamzin conceded.

"Still a lie," Laurence said. "I'll show you my sketch-book one day."

"Yes, do! Now?"

"Thought you were in a hurry for the stables!"

"Yes we are," Rissa said. "We promised to be there by ten so's to help with the water, and it's nearly that now."

"Well, I'll come up at tea-time," Tamzin said. "May I have my tea up here?"

"Better ask your mother; she's my nurse and knows what's good for me. Perhaps I mustn't be bothered!"

Tamzin wrinkled up her nose at him and followed Rissa out. Diccon met them in the hall, took Tamzin's hand and led her firmly to the larder door. He looked up hopefully and said, "More salt, Boy! Say please. Please!" all in one breath. Tamzin placed a tiny heap on the corner of the kitchen table, and Diccon pointed to the other corner and said, "Two salts, Boy!"

"Halve it," Rissa advised. "Shouldn't give him any more." So they halved it, and left him delightedly bouncing from one end of the table to the other saying, "*Two* salts Boy got! See dere!"

At the stables they nearly fell off their bicycles at the sight of Carillon's face looking over the door of the disused box. Miss Wade found them with their arms round his face and neck, rubbing their cheeks against his smooth chestnut coat.

"I'll bet he gave you a nice surprise!" she said.

"Surprise!" Rissa said. "He nearly gave me a heart attack, the darling horse!"

"Why is he here? Is he staying?" Tamzin questioned.

Mr. Randall appeared from Timpani's box with an empty bucket, set it down and came over. "I was on the 'phone to the vet after you'd gone yesterday," he said, "and he thought sea water would be the best thing now for Carillon's legs. George was bringing down some extra tackle for the gymkhana in the evening, so I gave him a ring and asked him to hitch on the horse-box and bring the old fellow down with him. We shan't use him of course, but we'll lead him down for his paddle every day and let him have a holiday in the paddock."

The horse hung his head low over the door in the bliss of having his ears gently stroked, and half-shut his eyes like a purring kitten.

"My word, but *aren't* you smart!" Mr. Randall said, suddenly noticing Tamzin's coat and jodhpurs.

"So this is the jumble sale get-up?" Miss Wade remarked. "Looks more like Saville Row to me."

Tamzin said, "Do you really think so? *Wasn't* it a windfall? And Rissa's will be finished to-night."

"Roll on Wednesday!" Rissa said, and gave Carillon a third piece of carrot. "His legs do seem to have gone down a bit," she observed, leaning over the door.

"Yes, I thought so too," Mr. Randall said. "I think he's going to get over it pretty well."

Joan Wade said, "We've got Miss Polkinghorne and the Hay boy in fifteen minutes. Better get on with the water."

They collected their buckets and the yokes and carried water for nearly fifteen minutes. "Never mind, they're always late," Miss Wade said, lowering the last bucket. Mr. Randall hung up the yokes and lifted the side-saddle on his arm. "You'd better take them, Joan," he said, "I want to get Carillon down to the sea early and then turn him out." He turned to the girls. "Cobweb will be the only one left in the stables, but you could share him for half-an-hour's gymkhana practice; you know what Saturdays are at Hillocks!"

The girls did this and were the first to leave the yard. Next went Roy Hay on Sea Pie, his immaculate aunt on Allegro and Miss Wade on the skewbald. Finally, while Rissa was cantering round the bending poles, Tamzin saw Mr. Randall on his white mare with Carillon walking stiffly by his side, heading down the track for the sea.

She sat on the top of the gate and watched Rissa take Cobweb over the jumps. "How well she holds her hands!" she thought. "I must try to keep mine as low as that; but Cobweb will be a different thing from darling Sea Pie. Gosh, I hope I remember about heels and don't upset him."

Rissa galloped up to the gate with a grin from ear to ear. "He's grand!" she said. "Once you get used to his funny ways he'll do anything for you." She patted his dappled shoulder lovingly and slipped from the saddle.

Tamzin mounted, a little doubtfully.

"And I think he's the most beautiful pony to look at I've ever seen," Rissa added. "He might have been painted with those round grey dapples, and his long white tail is quite perfect."

"It looks wonderful when he's galloping," Tamzin said. "Like a white silk streamer floating in the wind."

"M'm. Just think what it would be like if he were ours!"

"*Don't* think! It only makes you feel sad, and to-day is so perfect I don't want to feel sad." She squeezed her legs so gently the pony didn't notice them, and anxiously squeezed a fraction more.

"Don't be frightened of him; he'll know. Miss Wade says fear runs along the reins," Rissa cautioned, noticing.

"I'm not!" Tamzin said, bristling and suddenly determined as Cobweb moved into his long easy stride. She found him a joy to ride, to her surprise. Her aids were naturally much lighter than Rissa's and if anything she generally under-estimated the pressure. For a pony like Sea Pie her legs were inclined to be too light and not really effective, so with Cobweb she was almost perfectly mounted. She cantered round the poles with easy precision and headed her pony for the jumps. Feeling his punching rise from the hocks at the two-foot rail she tilted her weight forwards, dropped her hands and was cantering away on the other side before she knew it.

Rissa, watching from the gate, was a little stung to see how easily Tamzin handled this touchy pony at her very first trial. Compared with her own ups and downs it was remarkable. She pushed down the little jealous resentment as Cobweb cantered up to her, and flashed an admiring smile to Tamzin in the saddle. "You ride him much better than I do!" she said honestly.

"Don't be silly, Riss! But it is funny, I do really find him easier than Sea Pie. I mean he's much more responsive and seems to understand what I want so much better."

"Ought to swop, then. I expect my heels are a bit too heavy really, and I might do better on Sea Pie. We'll see what Mr. Randall thinks."

"All right, if you like. But never mind now, there's time for another round each if we're quick."

They changed places and Tamzin watched the dappled pony with a new sense of friendship and understanding. In her eyes he had become perfection.

CHAPTER ELEVEN

IT WAS about four o'clock when Tamzin propped her bicycle in the Vicarage shed. Mrs. Grey was knitting in a deck chair on the shady side lawn, and Tamzin went across and flopped lazily on the grass beside her.

"Had a good day?" her mother asked, changing needles.

"Heavenly!"

"Even on their busy Saturday? Did you get a good ride after all?"

"No, only half-an-hour in the paddock, and we shared Cobweb. My first time on him, Mummy, but he was so perfect he seemed like my own legs only faster. Then Carillon was there for sea water on his bruises, and it was lovely seeing him." Tamzin pulled blades of grass with her fingers and built them into a tiny stack. "Where's Diccon?" she said.

"Out with Daddy. Jodhs all right?"

"Oh, *yes*! And much more comfortable than shorts because they keep the leathers from pinching your legs. You do pack delumptious lunches, Mummy!"

Mrs. Grey counted to the end of her row and smiled. "Do I? And was that part of the heavenly day?"

"Of course. But all the day was nice; even the tack cleaning was fun to-day, and we had a gorgeous swim and lay in the sun to dry. It was sort of hot and dreamy and we talked about the gymkhana."

"It's very wise to know you're happy when you're

actually being happy," Mrs. Grey said. "And not just to look back and realise how happy you *were*."

Tamzin rolled on to her back and watched the drifting clouds through a canopy of apple-leaves. "I must be very wise then!" she said. "Because I know I'm happy, fit to bust, this very minute."

The gate clicked and Mrs. Grey said, "Postman I should think, unless it's Daddy and Diccon."

Tamzin sat up. "I'll go and see," she said. "And may I have my tea with Laurie, please? I won't make him tired."

"Yes, if he doesn't mind."

"Oh good!" Tamzin skipped across the lawn and round the house to the front porch. It had been the postman and there were three letters in the box. Two for Mr. Grey which Tamzin placed on the hall dresser, and one for Laurence Hunter. She bounded upstairs with this and took it to him. "It's just come," she said. "Is it the one you thought would come this morning?"

Laurence glanced at the envelope and said, "Yes, it's from home." He tore the letter open and began to read.

Tamzin sat on the window seat, picked up the *Daily Telegraph* and pored over the racing news to study the names of the horses.

Laurence looked up at her and said, "There's a bit here might interest you."

"Yes? Read it."

"Mother says, ' You remember the Framptons at Abbot's Hyde, who had a rather pretty child called Lesley? She still had ringlets when you were here last but she seemed to grow up a lot since she went away to school. Poor child, she's had a really bad accident, and may not be able to walk again for years, if at all. She was riding a pony her father'd given her last Christmas—a most lovely pure white creature that must have cost quite a lot—and fell at a jump in their own grounds. Mrs. Mills, who knows the Framptons quite well, told me the child's father was terribly upset and said the pony must be shot, although the gardener, who had seen the accident happen, said Lesley jumped the hedge under a tree and caught her head on a low branch, and that the pony couldn't be blamed in any way; it was an error on the part of the child. Mr. Frampton wouldn't accept this and would have had the poor beast shot at once, only Lesley kept asking after it and he was afraid of upsetting her.

" ' She'll never be able to ride it again, Mrs. Mills says, but won't hear of it being sold, and her father says he can't bear the sight of it and won't have it on the place or anywhere near him. So it does look rather as if he'll get his way in the end. It is a pity of course, because everyone says the pony is a really first-rate animal—an Anglo-Arab, or something— and quiet as a lamb. He only jumped where he did because Lesley rode him to it. She, poor child, fell awkwardly and hurt her spine. I do feel so grieved for the parents; they thought the world of her.' "

Laurence looked up from the letter and saw Tamzin staring frozenly at him over the *Telegraph*. "Go on!" she said in a small voice.

Laurence went on, " ' I am packing the pyjama jackets you wanted . . .' Oh, that's all about the pony." He finished the letter reading to himself, looked up again and saw that Tamzin was still staring over the *Telegraph* in an absent kind of way.

"Anything wrong, Tam?"

She looked dismally at him. "I just can't bear to think about it," she said.

"Well, don't, goosey!"

"I can't help it."

"Then you'll have to put up with it, my lass."

"Do you know this Mr. Frampton, Laurie? Should you think he really will shoot the pony?"

"I knew him pretty well. A most violent, unaccountable sort of chap I thought him. Shouldn't wonder at anything he did, really."

Tamzin lapsed into a depressed silence during which her mother brought in a tray of tea, looking curiously at Tamzin but only said would she help Laurie with his egg and remember he didn't take milk in his tea.

Tamzin carefully chipped the tops off the eggs, absently sprinkling a little sugar in each, and poured out Laurie's tea with milk in it.

"Now look here, Tamzin Grey, you haven't got your mind on your work!" Laurence said. "You've sugared my egg and milked my tea and next you'll be peppering the cake. What it is to be dependant on a wool-gathering pony-fan for your very meat and drink."

Tamzin looked contrite. "I'm sorry, I didn't mean to," she said.

The meal progressed one-sidedly with Laurence making conversational attempts and Tamzin scarcely noticing what he said or even that he was speaking at all. Suddenly she sat bolt upright, her downcast face transfigured in a flash to a glow of eager enthusiasm. "Laurie! I've had an idea!"

He put out a hand to steady his tea and said, "The deuce you have! Well out with it."

"The pony—would they let me keep him here, do

you think? Just till they'd made up their minds?
Oh *Laurie*! Would you write and ask them for me,
please?"

He studied her face, not having an answer ready.
She put her spoonful of egg down into her tea
without noticing and rushed on: "You said the
girl wouldn't let the pony be sold and the father
won't have it kept near him so if I had it here it
would suit everyone and oh, Laurie, I'd be so happy.
I'd just die of it!"

"Then a fat lot of good it would do you."

"Oh DON'T tease me now, Laurie, you can't
THINK what it all means to me. Oh PLEASE will
you help?"

He considered, grinding egg-shell with his
spoon. "I might," he said at last. "But you must
ask your mother first. She might have reasons
against it."

Tamzin jumped up. "Oh *darling* Laurie, will you?
May I take the letter now and show it to Mummy,
please?"

"Well, all right. It's this page." He handed a
sheet across the tea-tray and raised one eyebrow
humorously as she whisked out of the room.

Downstairs, Tamzin fidgeted restlessly while Mrs.
Grey read the fateful page over her last cup of tea,
and then passed it to Mr. Grey who was helping
Diccon finish his milk-cocoa. Tamzin was in an
agony of suspense till Mr. Grey looked up and said.
"Sounds a good idea to me. What do you think,
Gwen?"

Mrs. Grey was the practical parent, and pointed
out that they had chickens over most of the paddock
and Aunt Gabrielle's furniture stored in the stable.
So Mr. Grey said there was that, but he might find

another place for the chickens and why couldn't
Aunt Gabrielle store her furniture somewhere else
now, for a change? They'd had it for four years.
But Mrs. Grey said *he'd* have to write to her in that
case, and what about winter feed and bedding? The
pony was well bred and could hardly be expected to
live out.

Tamzin burst in with "Couldn't he have a New
Zealand rug?" and Mr. Grey said, "What was that?"
Mrs. Grey explained that it was a rug designed for
wear by a horse at grass, but was very expensive,
and Mr. Grey said it seemed to him Mrs. Grey was
only looking for difficulties instead of making the
constructive suggestions which he'd have expected
of her considering her own passion for horses, and
she retorted that it was *she* who had the worry of
making ends meet. This went on for some time,
like a game of mental tennis in which Tamzin was
the helpless ball-boy, running feverishly after everything they said. In the end they both decided that
Laurence could write the letter and they could worry
out the details if the Framptons accepted their
suggestion. Tamzin rushed from the room and
Mrs. Grey subsided into her chair. "And she said
she wouldn't tire him!" she said weakly.

The letter was written and posted, and Tamzin
lapsed into a state of anxious abstraction that even
the imminent gymkhana failed to lighten. Sunday
was just a torturous stretch of creeping time, and
Monday and Tuesday were interminable deserts of
existence, even though punctuated with all the long
anticipated final preparations from the Dunsford
Gymkhana. Their last practice rides in the Hillocks
paddock, the arrival of Rissa's jodhpurs, the final
immaculate cleaning of tack, and the polishing of

bits and buckles and irons till they shone like silver. Rissa was fairly boiling over with excitement and enthusiasm about everything, but Joan Wade remarked to Mr. Randall that Tamzin didn't seem to have her heart in anything but the future of the Anglo-Arab pony.

"She's all right," he replied. "It's only that she's torn to bits with suspense. Pity it's Yorkshire; day-and-a-half's post. She mightn't hear till after that Show, even if they reply by return."

Mr. Randall's decision that it would be a good plan to swop ponies with Rissa didn't produce more than a flicker of enthusiasm in Tamzin's abstracted mind.

There was no letter by the Wednesday morning, and Tamzin surprisingly made a sudden decision to batten down her gnawing anxieties for this one day and enjoy the gymkhana whatever happened.

The day began with rain and a fresh wind, but during breakfast the sky cleared fairly hopefully. Tamzin set forth blithely in her jumble riding outfit, now crowned with a brown felt hat with a turned-up-all-round brim.

Old Jim spat into the river and then into each hand before grasping his oars. "Don't see much of you around boats these days," he commented, swaying slightly to the oars.

"No, Jim," Tamzin felt an apology was being expected. "I love the boats just as much, of course," she added. "Only horses have *always* mattered most, and these are only here for such a short time."

"You allus was a downright honest 'un," Jim granted her dryly. "Fer my part I reckon 'osses best leave me be. Further I stays from they things comfortabler I feel."

"Yes, Jim, I expect you do. Will the sun stay out for us, should you think?"

Jim screwed up one eye and glanced windwards. "Be fine spells," he said. "But spit a drop too." He rowed in silence for a minute and by the steps suddenly said, "Lookee 'ere, Miss Tam, me and some more've put money on you fer to-day."

"You mean you've been *betting* on me, Jim?"

"Bin bettin', ah!"

Tamzin felt crushed by the responsibility of Westling men's money. How shocking if she lost everything, their money too. Though she knew her father's views about gambling and was quite genuinely shocked to think of herself as the subject of a private gamble.

"Well, I'll try my best, Jim," she said. "But you know I'm not very expert."

Jim spat again and grunted. "Ugh! You'll do."

Rissa was waiting at the lifeboat house, looking like someone entirely different. Tamzin thought at first that this was because she hadn't got used to Rissa in jodhpurs, and then suddenly realised that it wasn't.

"*Rissa!* You've cut your hair!"

"I know I have, drat you. It tickled and looked silly with jodhs."

"Oh, Rissa! I'm sure you could have made little plaits if you'd tried. And you'd got so far with it this time! What did your mother say?"

"She cut it. Likes it best short you know. But I do admit I'm a bit sorry now."

"You always are when you've done it."

"I know. Never mind. I can always grow it again. Any news about the pony?"

"Of course not. D'you think I'd even have noticed your hair if there was?"

Rissa shrugged. "All right! Don't bite me."

"Riss, do you really mind about not riding Cobweb? Honest?" Tamzin suddenly said.

"Well, I did at first but I don't now. I ride far better on the bay and Cobweb's made for you. We'll both have a better chance the way things are."

They rode into the yard, propped their bicycles and went towards voices in Ballerina's box. Looking over the door they saw Mr. Randall washing the white mare's legs while Joan Wade, perched on a stool, plaited her silky mane.

"Gosh! She does look marvellous!" Rissa said.

"What'll you do to her tail?" Tamzin asked.

"Probably nothing if time runs away like this," Miss Wade said. "Otherwise I might plait strands from the top."

"What can we do?" the girls asked, and Mr. Randall glanced up and said, "Nothing dirty in those clothes," and then, "What in thunder's happened to Rissa?"

"Her mother cut her hair," Tamzin said. "Isn't it awful?"

Miss Wade laughed. "She's been hogged for the gymkhana!" she said.

Rissa turned up her nose, and Mr. Randall glanced across to Tamzin. "No news?" he asked.

"Not yet. But could I plait Cobweb's mane, d'you think?"

"I dare say. Come in here and watch how it's done."

The girls sat on the manger and watched.

"Looks easy," Rissa said. "Only I'd be a bit scared of sticking the needle into the pony."

For the next half-hour they were absorbed with their plaiting and didn't even notice the clanking of buckets which announced that others were carrying water. The results were really good, and the ponies looked so smart the girls kept going back to admire them between combing all the horses' tails, polishing their coats with clean stable rubbers and blacking their hoofs with hoof-oil.

Joan Wade and Mr. Randall stepped out of dirty dungarees and revealed spotless breeches underneath. Saddles and bridles were sorted out and buckled on, the saddle-room locked and the yard gate swung open. Carillon tossed up his head as the horses filed out on to the track and Mr. Randall said, "Poor old chap! He hates being left behind."

The horse whinnied, arched his tail and trotted stiffly to the paddock gate, watching the string of horses moving down the track; Allegro first with Miss Wade, the ponies next and Mr. Randall following on Ballerina with the skewbald on a leading-rein.

No sign of the gymkhana was met with until the Hillocks string came out on the main road at the foot of the town. Along here they saw three children on ponies, a groom in charge of two heavyweight hunters, a woman riding side-saddle on a raking black gelding, and a couple of trailer horse-boxes.

Arriving at the field they passed through the competitor's gate and rode across to a quiet corner where the ponies and Timpani could be tied to the hedge. The two mares had not the temperament for such casual treatment and accompanied the party to the ringside. The programme had already begun, and tradesmen's turnouts were spanking smartly round the ring before the judges who were seated on chairs set on a dray by the entrance to the ring. Rissa began at once to decide which would be the first three, and Tamzin said, "Dunsford Dairy's got an entry, look!"

"So they have! It's Bessie, too."

"Well, Bonnie wouldn't be much good, would she? I can't see Bessie being in the first four, either."

Mr. Randall glanced at the programme. "Handy Hunters next. I'll get around to the collecting ring with Allegro if you'll take Ballerina, Joan."

Dunsford Dairies' Bessie was, as Rissa had guessed, not in it at all, and the first prize went to a very smart butcher's turnout from Hastings. Allegro's number was called fourth in the next class, just after the side-saddle woman on the raking black which they had passed on the road.

"Allegro'll have to do well to better her," Miss Wade said, standing at Ballerina's head. "She took first at Tonbridge last year. Almost perfect round this time too, except for rapping the gate."

Allegro did do well. Her jumping was faultless and she cleared the gate by inches. "Wait till she comes to the one she has to go *through*," Miss Wade said. "She's uncertain at that kind of job."

The chestnut stood for the gate to be opened but twice edged away before Mr. Randall had slipped the catch home.

"I thought she'd let her score down there," Miss Wade commented. "You two'd better get your ponies in the collecting ring for 'Child's best pony.'"

They were there and waiting before the last of the hunters was called. He stood among the children's ponies like a mastiff among terriers, a big grey weight-carrier with a Roman nose. The children trotted in after he had cantered away to the in-and-out beyond the ring. There were fourteen of them including Tamzin and Rissa, mostly strangers from neighbouring villages, but the girls recognised Judy and Jean Mattingley who lived in Dunsford but went to boarding school and rode New Forest ponies which were getting too small for them. There was a farmer's daughter called Maisie Hawkes whom Tamzin knew by sight and who rode a dun cob, both hogged and docked, and there were Dr. Hargreaves' twin sons on a smart bay and a breedy liver chestnut. The rest were just faces and unknown.

Tamzin and Rissa, being uncertain of the proper procedure, kept their ponies well behind the first six or seven and did what everyone else was doing or trying to do. When they got to cantering round the ring the two New Forest ponies wouldn't, but just trotted faster and faster, and the breedyliver chestnut hotted-up and went "all-abroad." An excitable black cob began to buck, left his rider on the carpet and bolted for the exit. Everyone else cantered round fairly happily but only five "collected" properly; they included the two Hillocks ponies and an old brown polo pony ridden by a boy in a checked coat and crash cap.

The figure-of-eight was the Waterloo of many including Tamzin and Rissa, who failed to get their ponies to change legs. Only the old polo pony and a small showy bay with a double bridle and fixed martingale completed the figure without a fault. The judges called in six ponies, including the polo pony, Cobweb, the bay with the double bridle and Sea Pie. The rosettes were handed out in that order, Sea Pie getting the white reserve. The other two, one of which was the Hargreaves' liver chestnut, went out of the ring and the four winners cantered once round and then away to be lost in the crowded field.

The judging for the Handy Hunters was now announced through the loud-speakers, Allegro coming second to the side-saddle black.

Wheelbarrows were trundled in for the next event, in which Miss Wade sat in the Hillocks barrow and Mr. Randall rode and led Ballerina. The two girls, left in charge of Allegro, watched from the ropes and laughed and cheered at the ludicrous sight of Mr. Randall tearing across the ring with Miss Wade in his barrow and Ballerina trotting disdainfully at his elbow. They were sixth out of an entry of ten and Mr. Randall, said afterwards, that he could have done better with the mare in the barrow and the girl in tow.

Hillocks Riding School had one sweeping success when Timpani and Ballerina carried off the first and second prizes in the Open Jumping, and Rissa surprised herself by actually winning the "Walk, Trot, Mount and Gallop," which she said afterwards must be due to Sea Pie's being such a perfect pony to lead. Cobweb held back at the turning posts and got Tamzin home last but one out of twelve. Neither of the Hillocks ponies were among the first four in Musical Chairs, which they found far more rough and difficult than they had expected, but the Bending Race was something for which they had practised carefully and often. Tamzin finished an easy first on the handy little grey, and Rissa just missed second place by inches.

The day ended in a soaking downpour with Hillocks horses wearing eight rosettes between them; three first, three seconds, a third and a reserve, and

Timpani had the challenge cup as winner of the
Open Jumping.

Everyone was streaming wet before they were
half-way home, but the girls at least were so blissfully content and so healthily tired that they scarcely
even noticed.

"D'you know, I almost *forgot* about Fallada
to-day," Tamzin said, in a shocked voice.

"Good thing too," Rissa said through the pouring
rain. "You'd have worried yourself sick and not
enjoyed the first gymkhana of your life."

"I know, but I can't help it."

"How do you know he's called Fallada, anyway?"

"He is to me," Tamzin said. "My pony was always
Fallada if he was white."

"Might have a name," Rissa objected. "And he
isn't your pony."

"Of course he will have a name! But it isn't his
proper name; his proper name is Fallada. And I
think he's *already* mine in some kind of way."

Rissa left it at that, and they jogged silently and
happily along.

CHAPTER TWELVE

THE LETTER came on the Thursday afternoon; Tamzin saw it in the hall when she came in from Dunsmere. She knew it was the letter because of the postmark and the strange writing and its being for Laurence Hunter.

"Mummy, it's COME!" she shouted, holding it.

"What's come?"

"The LETTER!"

"What letter?"

"Oh, MUMMY!" Tamzin was exasperated.

Mrs. Grey suddenly realised what her strange daughter was talking about and said, "Oh, of course! You mean from Mr. Frampton; let's take it up."

Tamzin held it out, suddenly feeling sick and cold. "You take it, Mummy, and tell me afterwards. I don't want to come."

"Not want to come?"

"I feel funny."

Mrs. Grey put out a hand and clasped Tamzin's fingers with the letter in them. "Come on!" she said. "You'll be all right."

They went upstairs, with Diccon puffing at their heels and Mr. Grey coming up behind saying, "Did you say Tamzin's letter'd come, my dear?"

They knocked and trooped into Laurence Hunter's room. The letter fell from Tamzin's fingers and she went to the window seat and hid behind the *Daily Telegraph*. Mr. Grey picked up the letter and gave it to Laurence. "Funny child, reading the paper when her letter's come," he muttered to his wife, and she said in a low voice "She's only nervous about it, Dick."

Laurence opened it and said should he read it aloud? Mrs. Grey sat down and said, "Yes, do, Laurie dear."

"It begins, ' Dear Mr. Hunter, Thank you for your letter. I regret I cannot possibly agree to your suggestion that my daughter's pony should be kept at Westling Vicarage.'"

Tamzin drew a sharp breath behind the *Telegraph* and bit her lip to stop its sudden quivering.

"' As you have apparently heard,'" Laurence read on, "' I wish to have the animal shot as the sight of it gives me considerable pain. My daughter's pleading for it, however, has prevented me from doing this, and I have suggested to her that it should be sold. She will not consider this proposal either, and I have had to make it quite clear to her that I cannot permit the animal to remain at Abbot's Hyde. She herself is willing for it to be lent to the child you mention, but you will understand that I cannot continue to be responsible for the pony's actions, and I made this plain to Lesley. She is fond of the beast and cannot appreciate that he is in any way dangerous, or responsible for her plight. In fact, she actually attempts to shoulder the blame for the accident, herself.

"However, she eventually agreed that the pony could be sent to Miss Grey on my conditions, as the alternative to its destruction; i.e., that I, from hence-forward, take no further responsibility for the animal's damages and that the ownership is irre-coverably transferred from the Frampton family to the Grey family. My daughter does not wish for any payment to be made, but only that the pony should be well cared for and retained permanently in the keeping of the Grey family.

'Awaiting your early reply. I remain, yours faithfully, Joseph R. Frampton. P.S. There are the following items:

" 'One white Anglo-Arab pony, "Cascade." 14.2 hands.

" 'One leather head-collar and rope.

" 'Two stable rugs.

" 'Grooming equipment.

" 'One snaffle bridle.

" 'One double bridle and running martingale.

" 'One Whippy hunting saddle.

" 'I wish for all the pony's effects to go with it.'"
Laurence looked up. "That's all," he said.

Everyone looked at Tamzin, except Diccon who was making a train with Laurence's grapes. She was still behind the *Telegraph*.

"Tamzin darling, isn't it just wonderful for you?" Mrs. Grey said, looking at the outspread newspaper.

"Y-yes," a quavering voice replied, followed by a loud and long sniff. Laurence pushed a handkerchief under the *Telegraph* and Tamzin dropped the paper and blew her nose. "I'm n-not crying because I'm s-sad," she said. "I j-just can't he-help it. Really I'm s-so happy I could b-burst," gulp.

"I know, darling! And the letter did begin on a rather hopeless note," Mrs. Grey said reassuringly.

"And now I suppose I'll have to write to Aunt Gabrielle," Mr. Grey sighed. "Though really, Gwen, I don't know if you think we aren't being very rash? Having a pony of this character for Tamzin I mean? Wouldn't a nice little forest pony suit her best? I mean, we don't want *her* involved in any nasty accidents, do we my dear?"

"Now, Richard, don't begin having doubts at *this* point. Surely you don't really think the Frampton child's accident was in any way the pony's fault? After what the gardener saw? And in any case you know quite well we can't buy a forest pony, or any other pony for that matter."

"Yes, quite, dear, quite. But this Mr. Frampton seems to think the animal rather dangerous; what do you think, Laurence my boy?"

"I, sir? I think the pony's all right. It's the old man who's a bit queer. Wants to believe the worst of it and does. Wants to blame something, I dare say, and the pony's what he's picked on; a sort of scapegoat, if you see what I mean."

"Yes, yes, of course! That is quite likely. Well, Gwenda, my dear, I will leave the matter to your judgment. It was always sound in regard to horses, I do admit. Perhaps I'd better drop a line to Aunt Gabrielle before the post goes."

He picked up Diccon and carried him from the room. Mrs. Grey replaced the grapes in the dish and said, "Well, Laurie, I should think you could write to Mr. Frampton that we shall be pleased to accept his offer. It is good of you to do all this for us!"

"Well, of course, you haven't been doing anything for me," Laurence said, smiling at her.

"Don't be silly, Laurie! You know we like having you, and no one could be less trouble. Come and help me get tea, Tamzin, will you? And afterwards we'll move the chickens to the tennis lawn."

Five days later Tamzin and Rissa were sitting on

the Vicarage gate reading a tattered old copy of *Horse and Hound*. They had been there for nearly an hour and it was still only half-past five. Every two minutes they glanced quickly up the village street and then bent again over the flapping pages stretched across their knees.

"He might easily get here a bit *before* six," Tamzin said. "After all, it must be difficult to judge one's time *exactly*, all the way from Yorkshire down to here."

"Might even be late," Rissa said. "Punctures and breakdowns and all that. Stable looks smashing doesn't it? Kind of welcoming, with the feed in the manger and hay and everything. Just think of him in it!"

"Just think! And it was full to busting with Aunt Gabrielle's stuff only yesterday morning!"

"We did have fun getting it all ready; I'm almost sorry we've finished it, aren't you? And it seems a pity in a way that he isn't really going to live in it till the winter."

"Much better for him to be out in warm weather," Tamzin said decisively. "You know Mr. Randall said stabled horses have twice as many illnesses and things as grass-kept ones. I shall put him out a lot in the winter too, if I can get a New Zealand rug."

"You could I expect, with your gymkhana money."

"I think that ought to go towards his keep. He'll cost a lot in the winter, and there's always shoeing."

"HE'S COMING!" both girls yelled at once, as a shiny black car appeared round the church bend with a horse-box swaying gently behind it.

She stared at him unbelievingly for a moment.

They leapt down, swung open the drive gates, ran to meet the shiny car and jumped on to the running boards. "That's the gate. I'm Tamzin Grey and that's Rissa Birnie. Is Cascade all right? I can't believe he's really in there behind!" Tamzin said all in a rush to the chauffeur at the wheel.

"Oh aye, he's all right, Miss. Tired, I dare say; bin on the road all of ten hours." He swung the car expertly through the gates and down to the front door.

"You can turn right round here when you want to get out," Tamzin said. "Can the pony come out now?"

"Oh aye, if you've got a place ready." The chauffeur backed out of the car and straightened up. "Makes yer stiff, drivin' all day," he said.

"We've got a stable *and* paddock ready, though it meant the chickens going on the tennis lawn,"

Tamzin said. "Will you wait a minute while I call Mummy and Daddy, please?"

She ran into the house and out again almost at once with her family behind her. The chauffeur lowered the horse-box door to form a ramp to the ground and climbed up it into the box. Cascade, in a brown head-collar, was led down the ramp and the rope put into Tamzin's hand. She stared at him unbelievingly for a moment, then put out a hand to stroke his smooth neck. He pushed a soft muzzle against her side and she drew a small red apple from her pocket. He took it delicately and crunched it with quiet appreciation.

"Nice little 'orse, that," the chauffeur said in an aside to Mr. Grey. "Wouldn't 'urt a fly, 'e wouldn't. But the boss, 'e got 'is knife in 'im, in a manner er speakin' like. Might be a proper devil, the way 'e talks, but 'e ain't no more vice'n a kitten."

Rissa stood holding Diccon's hand and saying, "Yes, darling! Horsey!" to his excited remarks, and Mrs. Grey stood beside her husband silently appreciating the lovely little horse with her trained and critical eye.

Tamzin said, "First I must take him under Laurie's window for him to see. And then as soon as I possibly can I must ring up Hillocks."

"I'm sure Laurie would love to see him," Mrs. Grey said, and the chauffeur added, "'E'll lead perfect, Miss. Follers too, 'e do, without no rope, just like a little dawg. Nice class of 'orse, that."

Tamzin led the pony round the corner of the house, Rissa following with Diccon's hand in hers. In the middle of the shady side lawn they stopped and called "Laurie!" They could see him reading in his bed at the open window. He turned and smiled at them and called down, "I'm no judge of horseflesh, but from an artist's point of view I should say he's as near flawless as mortal creature can be."

Tamzin flashed him a warm look and called back, "We'll come up when we get in!"

They turned back to the car where the chauffeur was unloading saddlery and equipment into the porch. "Shall you be wantin' these took round to stable?" he asked. "I'll tote 'em along fer you."

"I'm going there now, to give him a drink and a feed," Tamzin said.

"Put the little boy up on 'im, Miss, and give 'im 'orsey-ride. Gentle as a dove, that pony."

Rissa lifted Diccon on to the smooth rounded back and the procession went round to the stable with Mr. Frampton's chauffeur following under a load of Cascade's belongings. Rissa showed him where to put them all while Tamzin stood and stared at her beautiful Fallada, miraculously drinking *her* water in the stable she and Rissa had prepared for him.

Mrs. Grey took Diccon in her arms and said to the chauffeur, "You will come in and have a meal, won't you? You must be tired and hungry after your long drive." To Mr. Grey she whispered, "Let's leave them here with the pony, Dick. They've dreamed of this all their lives."

The two girls watched adoringly while the pony ate the meal they had put ready in the manger for him.

"He's more beautiful than anything I've ever seen in my life," Rissa said slowly.

Tamzin glanced at her and said, "That goes for me, too. And Riss—when Hillocks have gone away

we'll share my Fallada until your own pony comes.
And he will, I'm sure he will! Aren't you?"

Rissa slipped her fingers through the pony's mane
and said. "Yes, I think he will, too."

THE END